The Destroyer 40

Warren Murphy

DANGEROUS GAMES

PINNACLE BOOKS   LOS ANGELES

DESTROYER #40: DANGEROUS GAMES

Copyright © 1980 by Richard Sapir and Warren Murphy

An original Pinnacle Books edition, published for the first time anywhere.

First printing, May 1980

ISBN: 0-523-40714-9

Cover illustration by Hector Garrido

Printed in the United States of America

PINNACLE BOOKS, INC.
2029 Century Park East
Los Angeles, California 90067

FAIR GAME

Mullin screamed and before Sorkofsky reached the far wall, two of the blacks tackled him. As he fell to the floor, he released Mullin. When he shook his head and cleared it, he saw the Englishman standing in front of him.

"On your feet, ox," the Englishman said. "I won't even need a knife for you."

His one arm useless, Sorkofsky rose to his feet. As he did, Mullin reached out and kicked the hard toe of a pointed boot into the Russian's solar plexus.

Sorkofsky, instead of going down, roared and charged at Mullin, but as he reached the small Englishman, Mullin twisted his knife upward into the Russian's stomach, and Dimitri Sorkofsky fell to the floor, his eyes already glazing over.

The room was as quiet as death.

"Well done, lads," Mullin said, although it had not been as easy as he had anticipated or would have liked. The big Russian was a bloody bull and had made things more difficult than they should have been. Still, the terrorists' point had been made. The security officers for the Olympic Games were dead. The world would know the terrorists were not joking.

The telephone rang on the small phone ledge behind the spot where Sorkofsky's desk had stood.

Mullin said quickly, "All right lads, let's go." As they went out the door, he added: "The American is next. This Remo. . . ."

THE DESTROYER SERIES:

CHAPTER ONE

He was known throughout Greece as The-Tree-That-Would-Not-Fall, but his real name was Miros. His arms were as big around as most men's legs, and his thighs were as thick as a horse's throat. He was forty-four years old, but he had tasted neither wine nor woman and the lumpy muscles of his stomach jutted through his skin like half-submerged stones rippling the surface of a slow-moving stream.

He was a hero, not only in his own village of Arestines but throughout all Greece. Still, as a child, his life had been dedicated to the glorification of the great god Zeus who, legend said, had begun the Olympic games in a battle against a lesser god for possession of the planet Earth; so, instead of living the life of an honored wastrel with a marketable skill, Miros lived a life normal to Arestines. Every day he went down into the caverns and brought up giant buckets of coal for the people of his village, to help warm them against the chill Aegean winters. The only break from this routine, day in, day out, summer and winter, was his visit to a fertile Greek plain every four years, to defend his Olympic wrestling title.

Now he was attempting to win his sixth title. He knew that that was as many as Milo of Croton had won a century before . . . and Miros of Arestines allowed himself the satisfaction of hoping that four years hence, he would be back to win his seventh

Olympic crown. No man had ever done that. It would be a record that would live for many years, long after Miros himself had turned to dust and his immortal spirit had been swept up to live with Zeus forever on Mount Olympus.

Miros sat on the earth inside his tent and shook his head to clear it of such thoughts. Before he could celebrate winning seven championships, he had better make sure he won the sixth. And there were his knees to worry about.

He had just begun to wrap the thin linen straps around his right knee when a man entered the tent. The man was tall and thin and his face pale and pink, an unusual look in this village, which had been peopled for the last week by athletes from all over Greece, sturdy men, nut-brown from working in the sun.

"Worried about your knees, Miros?" the thin man said. He was in his sixties, and he showed his years, and as Miros looked up at him, he realized sadly that Plinates was old. Plinates had been the head of the Council of Elders ever since Miros had been a boy, and now the thin man had grown old in the service of the village. Miros was glad he did not have to work with his head, but labored instead with his arms and legs and back. Plinates looked as if he were going to die soon.

Miros grunted no reply at all.

Then he realized that was rude and he said, "I am dedicated to the service of Zeus, but when he created men, he could have given a little more thought to their knees."

Miros spoke slowly and continued wrapping his right knee with the linen bandage. "No matter how big a man may grow, he has exactly the same knees as a little man. It does not seem to me to make much sense." He added quickly, "But of course, Zeus does not confide his plans to me."

3

Plinates grunted and sat on a cushion across from Miros as the dark-haired giant continued to wrap. First seven strips of linen from left to right. Then four strips of linen, vertically, along the length of the leg. Then four more strips from right to left. Finally, thin linen laces to hold the bandage in place. Then the left knee.

"I have seen your opponent," Plinates said. "He looks very strong."

"He *is* very strong," Miros said. "Ottonius is very strong. But he is a boy and I am a man."

"You were not much more than a boy when first you were victorious here," Plinates said. "One must beware of boys. They call this one The Knife."

"In these games, I am wary of everyone," Miros said without looking up. "That is why I wrap my knees."

"Perhaps it is the year that The Knife will chop down The-Tree-That-Would-Not-Fall," Plinates said.

Miros looked up quickly. If Plinates had not been the head of the Council of Elders and the best friend of his late father, he would have told the older man to leave the tent. But that would be disrespectful. He looked back down and resumed wrapping his left knee.

"Perhaps you are not ready," Plinates said.

"Not ready?" Miros said. It almost seemed as if Plinates was taunting him. "Not ready? Today, Plinates, I could wrestle the world and win. Not ready?" He laughed, a heavy, deep laugh that filled his barrel chest with air.

"That is too bad," Plinates said.

Miros looked up in surprise, dropping his linen wrappings to the dirt of the tent floor.

"Because today you are going to lose," the older man said. His pale blue eyes stared calmly at Miros, and the wrestler searched them for the sign of the

4

jest he was sure must come. But there was no jest. Plinates was serious.

"What are you talking about?" Miros said.

"You are going to lose today. The Council of Elders has decreed it."

"Fortunately," Miros said, "the council's ways are not my ways and council edicts have very little to do with wrestling."

"That is true," Plinates said. "This edict has nothing to do with wrestling. It has to do with government and with war. You will lose."

"But why?" Miros asked. He still did not understand. "So Ottonius of Kuristes is strong. And he is young. But he is also arrogant and foolish and he spends his life loosely on women and wine. He will never beat me."

"True enough," Plinates said. "But nevertheless he will win."

"How?" Miros asked.

"Because you will let him," Plinates said.

Miros rose to his feet angrily, the sound in his throat nothing so much as a growl. A lesser man would have fled the tent at the sight of the expression on his face. But Plinates neither moved nor showed emotion.

"You may thank Zeus that you were my father's friend," Miros said softly. His dark eyes flashed anger, and the cords in his neck stretched at their covering of skin. His big fists clenched and unclenched.

"Yes. I was your father's friend and I am your friend. But I am also the Chief Elder of the village of Arestines and that is my responsibility, even more than friendship."

"Yes," Miros said. "And our village has been fighting the village of Kuristes for five years and now we have a truce for these games and then today I will beat Ottonius of Kuristes and tomorrow we will be at

5

war again with Kuristes. Just as we always have. I fight for our village and our honor."

"How many have died in these five years of fighting?" Plinates asked.

"I don't know. I leave counting to politicians."

"Two hundred and six," Plinates said. "And now, if I tell you that you have it in your power to save perhaps another two hundred? Or four hundred? That you have it in your power to end this war? That you alone can make your village the victor? Then what do you say?"

"I say I am a wrestler," Miros said.

"And I say you are the son of a father who gave his life for the village of Arestines. Do you deny the value of what he did?"

And slowly Miros sat down on the dirt of the tent floor. He kicked away the linens with which he had been wrapping his left knee. He would not need them this day. He knew that and the truth lay in his stomach, as black and as hard as a giant lump of the Arestines coal he had mined for the past thirty years.

That afternoon, Miros of Arestines met Ottonius of Kuristes in the final championship match of Olympic wrestling. The hot Greek sun had coated both their bodies with sweat as they faced each other across the twenty-foot rectangle that had been scored in the earth of the plain, formed where the Cladeus and the Alpheus flowed together.

Ottonius was as tall as Miros, but he was as blond and fair-skinned as Miros was dark. Miros had seen Ottonius pin his opponents in four other matches, and he knew the young man was skillful. But he also knew that he was stronger than Ottonius and faster and that he took better care of his body. What had Plinates said? That Miros wasn't ready? Not ready? He could pin a hundred like Ottonius this day.

Ottonius sneered at Miros and the older man wondered if Ottonius knew what Miros had been asked to do. Then he saw Ottonius glance down toward Miros's dark and heavy genitals, and decided Ottonius knew nothing, either about Plinates' demand or about genitals. If genital heft were the measure of a wrestler, then surely the bull of the fields would be the greatest wrestler of all.

The audience quieted as the referee signalled time and the two naked wrestlers moved warily toward each other in the center of the twenty-foot square. As they circled, Miros saw that Ottonius moved improperly to his right. The blond man stayed classically high on his toes, but when he moved to his right, he put too much of his weight on that foot and came down off his toes. It was not much but it was enough.

The two wrestlers came together and locked hands. Miros took two steps to his right, forcing Ottonius to circle to his right to keep facing his opponent. Miros felt Ottonius's steps. One. Two. Just as Ottonius planted his weight again on his right foot, Miros threw his own weight back to the left, fell onto his back, planted his right foot in Ottonius's belly and tossed the big blond up in the air, over his head. Ottonius landed on his back with a thump. Dust exploded in the air as his body hit. Before he had a chance to scramble to his feet, Miros was on him. He wrapped his arms around the blond man's neck.

"Don't you ever sneer at me, you son of a Kuristes dog," Miros hissed in the younger man's ear. Ottonius struggled fiercely to free himself from the head lock, but his movements just seemed to burrow his head and neck deeper into Miros's giant arms.

"You move like an ox," Miros hissed softly. "That is why you lie here like a sheep for shearing." He tightened his hold around Ottonius's throat, and the man from Kuristes tried to kick up into the air with his feet so his weight would slide his sweaty head out of Miros's arms. But the maneuver failed.

"And you wrestle like a woman," Miros said. "I

7

could hold you like this until you go to sleep. Or I could just simply move my arms and snap your neck. Do you understand?"

Ottonius tried to wriggle loose. Miros tightened his hold still more and twisted his body slightly sideways so that his weight put pressure on Ottonius's neck. The blond could feel his head starting to pull away from his spine.

"I said, do you understand?" Miros demanded.

"Yes," Ottonius said. "Yes."

"Very well," Miros hissed. "Now, you giant clod, I am going to let you go without killing you, but try to wrestle well enough to make it look believable. Kick out with your feet again."

Ottonius kicked both feet up into the air. This time Miros loosened his grip and Ottonius slid out from his arms. As the younger man scrambled to his feet, Miros dove across the ground at him. He made himself come up inches short. He lay on his face in the dirt. He felt Ottonius jump onto his back and wrap his arms around Miros's throat.

"Why?" Ottonius asked as he lowered his face toward Miros's ear. "Why did you do that?"

"I don't know," Miros said. "Perhaps I just wasn't ready today." He let Ottonius hold him for a reasonably long time before he raised his hand in surrender. Ottonius stood up, raised his hands over his head in a gesture of victory, then reached down to help Miros to his feet.

Miros got up by himself. "I don't need your help, you peacock," he hissed. The audience still sat silently, stunned by the swiftness of the victory, but they cheered minutes later when Ottonius received the gold medal on a chain. Miros stood alongside his opponent and praised Ottonius's strength and quickness. Ottonius praised Miros's skill and called him the greatest champion of all time. It made Miros feel good, but not good enough.

Back in his tent, Miros found a small bag that Plinates had left. In it were six gold pieces. It was a fortune, designed to make Miros feel better about losing. He went to the river and threw the gold pieces in.

Ottonius led his delegation of athletes home that night to their village of Kuristes. He had already forgotten the peculiar circumstances of his victory that afternoon, and he swaggered at the head of the athletes' line like Achilles marching around the walls of Troy. As they neared the walls of Kuristes, the other athletes lifted Ottonius onto their shoulders. It was the signal the villagers had waited for.

Using heavy hammers, they began to chop a hole in the wall surrounding their village, because the tradition that had come down through the ages said: with such a great champion in our midst, who needs fortifications to defend against enemies? It was a tradition as old as the Olympic games themselves, said to have come from the land of the gods far across the seas.

The Kuristes athletes stopped in front of the hole in the wall. On a hilltop, a hundred yards away, the dark-haired Miros of Arestines sat and watched, shaking his head sadly, finally understanding.

Ottonius postured in front of the wall, marching back and forth, inspecting the hole. Up on the hill, Miros could hear his voice complaining.

"I have vanquished Miros of Arestines," Ottonius bellowed. "Is this tiny little crack what you think I deserve?"

Even as he spoke, men with hammers made the hole in the wall wider and higher. Finally, it was large enough for Ottonius to pass through without stooping. The other athletes followed him. Soon darkness covered the land, but inside the village, fires burned and there were sounds of singing and dancing.

9

All night, Miros sat on the hilltop watching. The noise stopped two hours before daybreak. Then, as he had expected, he saw a group of men, dressed in full battle gear, scurrying over a hill toward the village.

That would be Plinates leading the men of Arestines, Miros knew. The troop passed unchecked through the hole in the wall of Kuristes. Soon, screams rent the air that had resounded with music only a few hours before. By dawn, the village of Kuristes had been slaughtered down to the last man, including Ottonius, Olympic champion wrestler.

On the hilltop, Miros stood. He sighed heavily, thought of all the dead inside the village of Kuristes, and wiped a tear from his eye. The Olympic games had been made an instrument of war and politics, he realized, and they would never again be the same.

It was time to go back home and get to work in the mines. He walked away and into the dim mists of Olympic history.

The lesson he had learned—to keep politics out of the games—would be largely heeded until, twenty-five centuries later in a city called Munich, a gang of barbarians would decide to make a political point by killing innocent young athletes. The world's horror and revulsion at this act was short-lived, and soon the terrorists were the adopted darlings of the left-looking, and others thought to copy their tactics—in a city called Moscow. In a country called Russia. In the 1980 Olympic games.

Jimbobwu Mkombu liked to be called "president" and "king" and "emperor" and "ruler for life" of what he vowed would one day be the unified African nation that would succeed South Africa and Rhodesia on the world's maps. He certainly did not like to be called "Jim."

In deference to this preference, Flight Lieutenant

Jack Mullin, late of Her Majesty's Royal Air Force, did not call Mkombu Jim. He called him "Jim Bob," which he knew Mkombu did not like, but which he was sure Mkombu would prefer to Mullin's private name for him, which was "pig."

That this last name had a solid basis in fact was reinforced for Mullin when he walked into Mkombu's office in a small building hidden inside the jungle, just across the Zambia border. The entire desk top in front of Mkombu was covered with food, and the food was covered with flies. This did not discourage Mkombu, who ate with both hands, shovelling food into his face and swallowing any of it that did not manage to drop onto his bare chest. Flies and all.

Mkombu waved a grease-covered hand at Mullin as he entered the office. In the same motion, he picked up a bottle of wine, took a long swallow directly from the bottle, then offered the bottle to the Briton.

"No, thank you, sir," Mullin said politely, controlling his face tightly so that the revulsion he felt did not show on his face.

"Well, then, eat *something*, Jackie. You know I hate to eat alone."

"You seem to have been doing a pretty good job of it," Mullin said. Mkombu glared at him and Mullin reached out and picked up a piece of chicken between right thumb and forefinger. With luck, he could nurse this chicken lump throughout the entire meeting and then go back to his own cottage where he kept a supply of American canned foods, which was all he ever ate in the jungle.

Mkombu smiled when he saw Mullin pick up the chicken, but he kept staring until the Englishman took a small bite and began, reluctantly, to chew. Mkombu nodded.

"You know, Jackie, if you keep killing my men, I'm not going to have any left to fight my war with."

11

Mullin sat in a chair facing the desk and crossed his legs. He was not a large man, standing only five-foot-seven and weighing 150 pounds, but men did not often underestimate him twice.

"If they keep challenging my authority, they'll keep getting killed. It keeps the rest of them in line."

"Can't you just hit them on the head or something? That'll get their attention. Must you kill them?" Mkombu wiped his greasy hands on the front of his dashiki shirt. Then, as an afterthought, he began picking the food from his sparse brilloed chest hair and popping pieces of the debris into his mouth. Mullin looked away, through the window, out toward the clearing that was the main jumping-off point for Mkombu's People's Democratic Army of Revolutionary Liberation.

"They don't understand hits on the head," Mullin said. "They understand getting killed. If I can't do that, Jim Bob, one day they'll run off and leave you and we'll be without an army."

"But the man you killed was better than any other three men I had."

Mullin sighed, remembering how easy it had been to kill the six-foot-six, 260-pound sergeant. Mullin had removed his .45 automatic, his pilot's cap, and his black metal-framed glasses. As he reached over to place his glasses carefully on the ground atop his hat, the big man's eyes had followed him, and Mullin had kicked out with his left foot and with the hard heel of his boot stove in the other man's Adam's apple. The fight was over before it had begun. To make sure, when the man dropped, Mullin had smashed in the man's temple with the steel-tipped toes of his high regimental boots.

"If he was better than any other three men, we are in deep trouble, Jim Bob. He was slow and stupid. A soldier cannot be a soldier without a brain. The size

12

of the army doesn't win a war. Discipline, and at least enough brains to follow orders, do."

Mkombu nodded. He had finished policing his chest and again wiped his hands on his shirt. "You are right, of course, which is why I am paying you so generously to be my chief of staff."

He smiled and Mullin smiled back. *Underpaying me,* Mullin thought, but he was satisfied that his time would come. Patience was always rewarded.

Mkombu rose from behind his desk and said, "Well, stop killing everybody for a while." And then, as if to halt any further discussion, he said quickly, "To the business at hand."

"Which is?"

Mkombu clasped his hands behind his back and leaned forward slightly at the waist. "The Olympic Games," he said.

"What event are you entering?" Mullin asked. "International pie-eating?"

Mkombu stood up straight behind the desk. He was only two inches taller than Mullin but outweighed him by more than a hundred pounds. His shirt was covered with food stains, and a glob of grease glistened in his graying black beard. He smiled and Mullin saw gold and silver glistening inside the pink cavern of his mouth.

"If I did not know better, Jackie, I would think you don't like me," Mkombu said.

It was a direct challenge and Mullin backed off, content that the day would come when he would make his move, but it would not be just yet.

"Just joking, Jim Bob," he said.

"Fine. You joke all you want. Why don't you eat that chicken in your hand?"

He watched as Mullin brought it to his mouth and took another reluctant bite.

"All right," Mkombu said. "Now the Olympics."

"What about them?"

"The athletes from South Africa and Rhodesia may not be permitted to compete."

"So what," Mullin said with a shrug.

"It seems that might make both countries angry."

"Correct," Mullin said. "How does it concern us?"

"We are going to make what happened at Munich in 1972 seem like a picnic." He looked up and Mullin nodded. The Englishman knew the game. Mkombu would make short statements and Mullin would have to prod him with hows and whys and what-fors until the story was completely out. It fed Mkombu's ego to have the Britisher continually ask for clarification of his statements.

"How?" Mullin said.

"We are going to kill the athletes of one of the competing countries and place the blame on some white terrorist group from Southern Africa."

Mullin took off his glasses and inspected them in the light. He could play games too. He slowly replaced the glasses on the bridge of his nose and asked, "What for?"

"Once the deed is done in the name of the Southern African Somebodies for Something, the world will crack down on South Africa and Rhodesia. It will open the door for us."

"It didn't seem to work that way with the Palestinians. Everybody seems to have forgotten that they killed children at Munich. Why should they get upset about South Africa or Rhodesia?"

"Because South Africa and Rhodesia are anti-Communist," Mkombu said. "That guarantees that world opinion against them will be vicious and unforgiving. The Palestinians did not have that handicap."

Mullin nodded. "Might work," he said. "How many athletes will we be killing?"

"From this one country, every single one. All of them," Mkombu answered with obvious pleasure.

"And how will we accomplish this?"

14

"That, my dear Jack, is what I pay you so handsomely for. Figure it out. Naturally, we will be issuing threats in advance so we can begin turning public opinion against the white regimes. The mass murder will be the final touch."

"A minimum force, of course," Mullin said.

"Of course. The fewer people who know about it or are involved in it, the better." He sat back down again. Almost without directing it, his hand moved toward a piece of beef. A fly moved away as his hand closed in.

"One problem," Mullin said. "Your Russian friends. How are they going to like your messing up their Olympics?"

"If you do your job well, they will never know it was us," Mkombu said.

"All right," Mullin said. He stood and tossed the piece of chicken with the two small nips taken out of it back onto the desk. Mkombu, he was sure, would eat it later. Waste not, want not. He started to the door.

"You forgot something," Mkombu said as Mullin's hand turned the door knob.

"Yes?"

"Don't you want to know the country whose athletes we will be killing?"

"It's not really important, Jim Bob, but go ahead. What country?"

"A major power," Mkombu said.

"Very good," Mullin said. He refused to ask which one.

"In fact, the world's most major power."

"Whatever you wish, sir," said Mullin.

"The United States of America, Jack. The United States of America."

Mullin nodded impassively.

"I want all their athletes dead," Mkombu said.

"Whatever you want, Jim Bob," Mullin said.

15

CHAPTER TWO

His name was Remo and he never played games. So instead of climbing up the side of the Hefferling Building in Chicago as he would have if stealth had been required, he walked in the front door, off North Michigan Street, just a wolf-whistle away from the Playboy building. He walked past the guard to the bank of elevators in the back.

As he waited for the elevator, Remo wondered how much energy it consumed to carry people to the higher floors. He thought that people would be much better off if they walked, and it would help solve the energy shortage too. He thought about running up the fourteen floors to the office of Hubert Hefferling, president of the Hefferling energy group, as his personal contribution to solving the energy crisis.

Then he remembered why he was there and decided he was making a big enough contribution to America's energy problems, and when the elevator came and opened its door, he stepped inside.

Remo did not care about heating oil shortages or gas shortages because he did not own a house or a car. But there were people who did care, and it was for these people that Remo Williams was going to kill a man he had never met.

He walked past the receptionist inside the suite of offices on the fourteenth floor and presented himself to Hefferling's pretty young secretary.

"I've come to decimate Mister Hefferling. Is he in?" Remo said.

The secretary's name was Marsha. She was equipped with a full range of retorts for people who wanted to bother Mr. Hefferling about the gas shortage or the oil shortage—particularly the gas shortage—but when she looked up, all the retorts became lodged in her throat.

Not that Remo was exceptionally handsome, but he had dark hair and high cheekbones and deepset dark eyes that seemed to rivet her to her chair. He was about six feet tall and thin, except for his wrists which were like tomato cans.

Marsha opened her mouth to speak, closed it, opened it and closed it again. She got that feeling in her stomach that she got when she saw Clint Eastwood in the movies.

"Sir?" she managed to sputter.

"Hefferling. I've come to decimate him. Where is he?"

"Of course, sir. I'll announce you. May I have your name please?" she asked and hoped he would give her his address and telephone number too and wondered why this lean, dark man made her feel so . . . so . . . well, outright raunchy.

"Tell him that Everyman is here to see him," Remo said.

"Of course, sir. Mr. Everyman."

He leaned closer to her and said, "But you can call me Ev."

"Ev. Yes, sir. Of course. Ev. When can I call you Ev?"

"Anytime," Remo said.

"Tonight? Right now?"

"First Hefferling," Remo said.

"Right." She depressed the switch on the intercom, never removing her eyes from Remo's. He smiled and she felt herself blush.

19

"Yes, Marsha?" a voice crackled over the speaker. Remo leaned nearer her and listened in.

"Uh, Mr. Hefferling, there's a Mr. Everyman here to see you, sir," she told her employer.

"Everyman? What the hell kind of—? Does he have an appointment?"

Remo smiled and nodded his head and as if hers were attached to his, Marsha began nodding too and she lied to her boss and said, "Yes, sir. He does. Something about decimals, I think."

"Decimals? What—? Oh, crap, send him in."

"Yes, sir." She clicked off the intercom and told Remo, "You can go in."

"Thank you. Your name's Marsha?"

"Yes. And I live alone," she said, the words coming out in a rush.

"I'd like to talk to you when I come out of Mr. Hefferling's office. You still be around?"

"Absolutely. I'll be here. I'll wait. I won't go anywhere. Promise. I'll be right here."

"Good. Wait for me."

"I will. I promise."

She buzzed Remo into Harold Hefferling's office. He waved to her before entering.

When the door closed behind him, he looked at the man seated at the desk.

"You Hefferling?" Remo asked.

The man was frowning at his appointment book.

"I knew it," he said triumphantly. "You don't have an appointment, Mister Whatever-your-name-is. How much did you give that bitch to let you in? I'll fire her ass right out of this building, boobs or no boobs."

Remo walked toward the desk and the man behind it stood up. Harold Hefferling was in his forties and kept himself in excellent shape. At six-feet-two and two hundred pounds, most of it muscle, he had even taken some karate lessons since the gas shortage, because people who recognized him on the street sometimes gave in to their desire to take his head off, over their frustration about gas shortages. Apparently, his standing up was meant to intimidate the smaller Remo.

"You," he said, pointing. "Out the same way you came in and take that piece of fluff out there with you." Remo reached out and took Hefferling's index finger between his own right index finger and thumb and told the bigger man, "Don't point. It's not polite."

Although he had no desire to sit down, Harold Hefferling did and abruptly. He looked at his finger. It did not hurt but it seemed to have had something to do with his sitting down.

"Who the hell are you?" he demanded of Remo.

"I told your secretary," said Remo as he perched on the edge of Hefferling's desk. "I am Everyman. I speak for Everyman. If I opened my shirt, you would see a big red 'E' tattooed on my chest and it would stand for Everyman."

"You're nuts," Hefferling said. Suddenly, for a moment, he was frightened. The man was obviously a lunatic, maybe one whose brain had gone soft from spending too many hours in too many gas lines under too much hot sun. He decided to take a softer tone. "Well, what do you want, Everyman? Something about decimals?"

"No," Remo said. "She got that wrong. I said I wanted to decimate you. But I don't want you to think I'm unreasonable. So first you tell me why you make this gas shortage worse and then I'll decide whether I'm going to kill you or not."

Hefferling's mouth dropped open. He made a sound that sounded like "glah, glah." He tried again and it came out clearer. "Kill, kill?"

"Just once," Remo said. "Kill."

"You are nuts," Hefferling said. "Stark, raving mad."

"Mad? We're all mad. We're mad because we have to sit on gas lines, because people are killing people on gas lines and the only line you see is the one at the bank when you deposit your money. Mad? Sure. We're fed up and we're not taking it anymore." Remo smiled. He had heard that line in a movie and always wanted to use it.

"But you're wrong. Dead wrong." Hefferling paused and reconsidered the phrase. "I mean, you're wrong. There *is* a shortage and it's the fault of the Arabs, not me. Honest, Mr. Everyman."

"You can call me Ev," Remo said.

Hefferling was sweating. He closed his eyes as if he were trying hard not to cry.

"Look, Ev, you just don't understand."

"Explain it to me," Remo said.

"Will you please let me talk?" Hefferling screamed. He jumped to his feet. Remo wondered if the room was soundproof.

"Sit down," he advised. Hefferling blinked rapidly, convincing himself that he didn't have to sit down if he didn't want to. After all, whose office was it and who did this Everyman think he was? Remo touched his chest and he sat down.

"Okay now, go ahead," Remo said. "Explain."

Hefferling's eyes rolled as if on the inside of his eyelids was written what he should say. What could he tell this madman?

"Look, it's true. Some people are making this shortage worse." That was good, he thought. It was the truth. He had read somewhere that you shouldn't lie to a crazy man. Maybe if he told him the truth that he wanted to hear, then, maybe this nut would believe everything he told him. Remo rewarded this theory with a smile.

"These people buy up oil on the spot market but

22

then they hold it, waiting for prices to go higher before they sell it in this country. They asked me to join them, but when I heard about it, I walked out. I wouldn't have anything to do with that. I said their plan was un-American."

Remo nodded. "Good for you," he said. "And you wouldn't have anything to do with it."

"That's right."

"Because it was un-American."

"Right. Right."

"And you are a loyal American."

"I am."

"And you don't care one bit about making a few extra million dollars."

"Right. I don't."

"Come on, Hefferling," Remo said reproachfully.

"It's the truth."

"That's your defense? That's supposed to stop me from killing you?"

Hefferling stared at him. Slowly his face relaxed into a smile.

"I get it. This is a joke, isn't it? You were paid to do this, right? Kind of like a pie in the face. Paid for it, right?"

Remo shrugged. "Actually, I was. But, see, that's the work I do."

"What is? Pies? Threats?"

"No," Remo said, and because it no longer made any difference, he told Hefferling the truth. How a young Newark policeman named Remo Williams had been framed for a murder he didn't commit, was sent to an electric chair that didn't work, and was revived and recruited to work for a secret crime-fighting organization named CURE. And he told him, too, how Remo Williams had learned the secrets of Sinanju, an ancient Korean house of assassins, and in learning them had become something more than just a man. Something special.

23

When Remo was done, he looked at Hefferling's face but saw only confusion there. Nobody ever understood.

"Anyway, Hefferling, upstairs tells me what is what here. I don't even use gas. But they tell me you have five tankers of oil tied up in Puerto Rico somewhere and you're waiting for prices to go up and then you're going to sell the oil in America. Meanwhile, people are waiting in gas lines. This is what upstairs tells me and they tell me I should do something about it."

"Like what?" asked Hefferling.

"Like kill you."

"Wait now," Hefferling pleaded in panic. "I've got more to tell you. A lot more. Wait."

"Tell it to the angels, Hubert." Remo leaned forward, tapped once with his knuckles and Hefferling sat back in his chair. Remo picked up the man's right hand, and dropped it onto the table with a thud. A dead thud.

"That's the oil biz, sweetheart," Remo told the body.

He walked around the desk, pulled a blank sheet of paper from the top left corner of Hefferling's desk, and found a Flair marker in the dead man's inside jacket pocket. In black, he wrote across the sheet of paper. With a piece of Scotch tape, he attached the paper to Hefferling's forehead, first wiping away the perspiration with a piece of the man's desk blotter.

He folded Hefferling's hands across his lap. At the door, he turned back to survey his work. There was Hefferling's body, sitting up neatly. On the paper dangling from his head was written:

DON'T TREAD ON ME.
SUCH IS THE VENGEANCE OF
EVERYMAN.

When Remo walked back outside, Marsha turned anxiously toward the door. When she saw him, she smiled. *There it is again,* she thought, that feeling in the pit of her stomach.

"Hi, Marsha," Remo said.

"Hello. You wanted to . . . talk to me?"

"Actually, no, Marsha. I wanted to kiss you."

She felt herself getting dizzy as he bent over her and placed a hand between her shoulder and her neck. She waited anxiously for his lips to touch hers. She thought she felt his breath on her forehead and then there was a gentle pressure on her throat and she felt nothing more.

Remo placed her head gently on her desk, cradling it on her arms. When she woke, she would feel fuzzy and dazed and find it difficult to remember what had happened in the last half-hour. Later, she would tell police that she had fallen asleep with her head on her desk and had dreamed about a man, but she could not describe him, except to say that he made her stomach feel funny.

"I think your head is funny," one of the cops would growl, but he would write in his report, "No witness to Hefferling murder."

Remo walked back to his hotel room, strolling past the Playboy Club, where he waved at people sitting near the windows and yelled at them that they ought to be playing racquetball, instead of drinking so early in the day.

Back at his room, he walked up to an aged Oriental who sat in a lotus position in the middle of the carpeted floor. Remo said, "I am Everyman. Beware my vengeance." He pointed his index finger toward the ceiling for emphasis.

The Oriental rose in one smooth motion, like smoke escaping from a jar, and faced Remo. The old man was barely five feet tall and had never seen a

25

hundred pounds. At the sides of his head, white wisps of hair flitted out from his dried yellow skin.

"Come, my son, and sit," he said to Remo, guiding the young man forcefully to the couch. Remo didn't want to sit down. The old man gently touched his chest and Remo sat down.

The old man shook his head and said sadly, "I have been expecting this."

"Expecting what, Chiun?" Remo asked.

"The strain of learning the techniques of Sinanju has finally driven you mad. It is my fault. I should have known that a white man could not stand the strain forever, even with my genius to guide him. It is like trying to pour an ocean into a cup. Eventually the cup must crack. You have cracked. But remember this, Remo, before they come to take you away: you did well to last this long."

"Come on, Chiun. It was a joke."

Chiun had returned to the lotus position and appeared to be praying for Remo's memory, his hands folded across the lap of his purple kimono.

"Chiun, stop it. I'm not crazy. It was just a joke."

"A joke?" Chiun said, looking up.

"Yes. A joke."

Chiun shook his head again. "Worse than I feared. Now he jokes with the teachings of the Master of Sinanju?"

"Come on, Chiun, stop fooling around."

"My heart is broken."

"Chiun—"

"My spirit is low."

"Chiun, will you—"

"My stomach is growling."

The cartoon lightbulb flashed on over Remo's head. "Oh, crap. I forgot your chestnuts."

"Don't apologize, please," Chiun said. "It is nothing, really. I couldn't expect you to remember a sick

26

old man's request, when you had the chance of frolicking with those rabbits."

"What rabbits?"

"At that palace of evil."

Remo scrunched up his face, trying to remember what Chiun was talking about. "Oh. They're bunnies, not rabbits."

"I will pray for your salvation."

"Chiun, I promise you, I didn't even walk past that place."

Chiun snorted. "The promise of a white man who also promised to bring home chestnuts."

"The promise of a student of a Master of Sinanju, of the greatest Master of Sinanju," Remo said.

"I will believe you for all we have meant to each other," Chiun said.

Remo stood up, bowed from the waist and said, "I thank you, Little Father."

Chiun waved a hand magnanimously. "You are forgiven. Now go buy my chestnuts."

CHAPTER THREE

When the threat to the United States Olympic team arrived at the office of the Olympic committee, it was immediately brought to the office of R. Watson Dotty, head of the committee.

He was, however, otherwise occupied. He had heard that there was a swimmer in Sierra Leone who had accepted a free pair of bathing trunks from a swimsuit manufacturer, and Dotty was trying to pin down the rumor so he could demand the athlete's banishment from the upcoming Moscow games. It was Dotty's feeling that no one in the world but him knew the difference between amateur and professional, and he was dedicated to keeping the difference alive. So he pushed aside the note that was laid on his desk by his assistant.

"Better read it, Commodore," his assistant told Dotty.

Dotty looked up, annoyed at the tone of fiat in his assistant's voice, but picked up the note. It was hand-printed in block letters. It read:

"In protest at the harassment of athletes from South Africa and Rhodesia around the world, the United States Olympic Team will be destroyed. This is no idle threat."

The note was signed "S.A.A.E." and under that was printed "Southern Africans for Athletic Equality."

"Shall we take it seriously?" the assistant asked.

"How the hell should I know?" Dotty said. "I can't be bothered with this stuff. There's a swimmer in Sierra Leone and I know he's stealing commercial money. We have to protect our amateurs from him."

The aide wanted to say that he doubted the Sierra Leone's swimmer's graft would pollute the Olympic swimming pools, but contented himself instead with pointing out that perhaps American athletes should be protected against this threat from the S.A.A.E.

"Have you ever heard of this group before?" Dotty asked.

"No, Commodore."

"Neither have I. Dammit, why do people have to do things like this?"

His assistant didn't answer and finally Dotty said, "Forward it to the FBI by special messenger."

"The president too?" the assistant asked.

"Of course," Dotty said. "The White House too. Let them worry about it. I've got important things on my mind. Go ahead. Send them off."

When his assistant left the room, Commodore R. Watson Dotty, who had been awarded his military title by a yacht club in landlocked Plainfield, New Jersey, slammed his fist down on the desk.

Let it be a crank.

"Be nice if it was a crank," the director of the FBI said.

"We can't take that chance though, can we, sir?" asked the director of Special Operations.

"I should say not. And I guess we'll have to alert the White House."

"They already know, sir," the director of Special Operations said. "A copy was sent there as well as to us."

The FBI chief shook his head. "Did he send one to anyone else? The UN or the CIA or the *Washington Post*? God, doesn't the fool at the committee know we're here to handle these things? If we thought the president should be notified, we'd notify him."

"You've got one out of three, sir," the assistant said.

"What are you talking about?"

"The UN and the CIA didn't get copies but the *Post* did. So did the *New York Times* and all the TV networks. Seems the S.A.A.E. made enough copies to go around."

"Bloody nice of them, wasn't it?" the director said. He was of the opinion that when he said things like that, he sounded like Sir Laurence Olivier. He'd always wished that during the war he had served in Great Britain so he could have had an excuse to affect an English accent. "Bloody nice indeed," he repeated.

Wonderful, the president thought. *Wonderful. To inflation, unemployment, the oil crisis, and our overseas alliances falling apart, I can add the slaughter of the U.S. Olympic team. Reelection? I'll be lucky I don't get lynched.*

"Mr. President?" one of his staff said and he looked up in surprise from the note. He had forgotten they were standing there.

"The press wants a statement of some kind."

"It's a crank," the president said. "It has to be." *It better be,* he thought to himself. *I just don't need this.*

"I don't think that's the right tack to take with the press, though," his top assistant said.

"All right. How about this? We guarantee—absolutely guarantee—that nothing will happen to any of our athletes in Moscow. Try that. Absolutely guarantee. Make me sound like that football player in panty hose. You know what I mean. That might be good."

32

"Okay," the aide said. "We can do that."

"But check it with my wife first," the president said. "She might have some other ideas."

"She usually does," the press secretary muttered under his breath as he left the office.

His remaining aide said, "Shouldn't we do something about security?"

The president fixed him with his best I-was-just-coming-to-that glare and the man quieted down.

"I want the Russians notified that we have to be involved in the security arrangements. Our team's been threatened. They have to let us in."

"All right, sir."

"The FBI's working on this?"

"Yes."

"Okay, go do what I told you."

When the room was empty, the president brooded and thought about the no-dial telephone upstairs in the dresser in his bedroom.

The telephone connected directly to the secret organization CURE and its director, Dr. Harold W. Smith. The president's predecessor in office had explained it all to him. Smith had been tapped some years back to run the CURE operation. The idea was to work outside the Constitution to put the squash on crooks who were hiding behind the Constitution. But over the years, CURE's operations had expanded and now it was ready to go anywhere, to do anything. Every president, he was sure, had felt the same way coming into his office: he would never use CURE.

And just as he had, every one of them had wound up using it.

Not that it was easy. The president could not give CURE orders. He could only suggest missions. Dr. Smith was the final boss. There was only one order a president could give that would instantly be obeyed: disband. No president had ever done it because every

33

president had found that America needed CURE and Dr. Smith and the enforcement arm, Remo, and the little old Oriental who did the strange things.

The President of the United States went up to his bedroom and removed the receiver of the phone and waited for Smith to answer at the other end.

Why was the phone always so cold? he wondered.

CHAPTER FOUR

Dr. Harold W. Smith did not like to meet in public places. That was his position. Remo's position was that if Smith wanted to meet with him and Chiun, he would have to meet where Remo told him to.

And so, because he knew that Remo was quite capable of disappearing for three months without even a word, Dr. Smith found himself in a cable car high above the pedestrian walkways of the Bronx Zoo, trying to explain the latest problem to his two assassins.

"Really, Remo. The Bronx Zoo?" Smith complained.

"I like zoos," Remo said. "I haven't been to a zoo in a long time."

Chiun leaned close to Smith. "He is hoping to find some relatives, Emperor," he whispered loudly in Smith's ear.

"I heard that," Remo snarled.

Chiun looked up with an expression of bland innocence.

"And stop calling him emperor," Remo said.

Chiun seemed surprised. For thousands of years the Masters of Sinanju had contracted out their services to emperors, czars and kings of the world, and he thought it only fitting to refer to Smith as Emperor Smith. He said to Smith, "Ignore him. He is testy because everybody in the monkey house looks

36

exactly like him and he can't pick one relative from the next."

Smith pointed at the only other occupant of the cable car, a man asleep at the far end, sprawled across the seats. Remo and Chiun could tell he was stone drunk, because for them the fumes of his inebriation hung like thick fog in the car.

"He's out of it," Remo said. "Don't worry about it. So I'm supposed to babysit the entire Olympic team?"

"Foolish child," Chiun said quickly. "The emperor would not ask you to perform such an impossible task. This assignment seems most reasonable."

Remo looked at him suspiciously. He knew that Chiun generally thought that Smith was a lunatic because Smith resisted all Chiun's offers to eliminate the president of the United States and make Smith ruler-for-life.

And then Remo understood.

"Don't let him soft-soap you, Smitty. He wants to get over to Moscow for the Olympics so he can win a gold medal and go on television and get rich doing endorsements."

"Chiun?" Smith asked, leaning back and looking at the frail, aged Korean.

"Why not?" Remo asked. "He can win any event he enters. All of them, for that matter. So can I."

"For once you speak the truth, housefly," Chiun said. "He is right, Emperor."

"Well, Remo, you'll get a chance to prove it," Smith said. "The people in Moscow are being just about what you'd expect. Stubborn. They don't want any American security people in Russia. They figure they'll be CIA agents spying on them."

"We could send the whole CIA and they'd be lucky to find the Olympic Stadium," Remo said.

"If you want us to get secrets," Chiun started to tell Smith.

"I appreciate the offer, Master," said Smith. "I really do. Perhaps another time. Remo, you'll have to travel with the team as an athlete. But you'll have to work your way on through competition."

"You've got to be kidding," Remo said.

"This is wonderful," Chiun said. "If I can't go for the gold myself, who better than my own son?" He leaned close to Smith again. "He's not really my son because he's funny-colored, but I just say that to make him feel good." He leaned back. "Of course, I will travel with him."

"Of course," Smith said. "You can travel as his trainer."

"Perfect," said Chiun.

"This is a pain," Remo said.

"It will work out fine," Smith said. "Are you sure he's asleep down there?" He pointed again to the drunk at the end of the car.

"Out for the night," Remo said.

"What events shall we compete in?" Chiun asked Remo.

"I don't care. Pick one."

"You could win all the track events easily," Chiun said.

"Yeah," Remo said. "What've we got? The dashes, the hurdles, the 800 meter, the 1500, the mile, two-mile. There's the marathon, and . . . let's see, things like shotput, and pole vault, high jump, long jump. Aaaah, there's a lot of them."

"And gymnastics," Chiun reminded.

"Horse, parallel bars, rings, balance beam . . ."

"And be careful not to set any new world records at these qualifying contests," Chiun said. "That's not where the endorsement money comes from. Save the world records for the Olympics."

"Yes, Little Father."

"You can't possibly compete in all those events," Smith said, trying to regain control of the discussion.

"The brilliance of the Emperor," Chiun said. "Of course he is right, Remo. If you competed in every event, you would win every event, and so there would be no need to send an Olympic team."

"So? Then I wouldn't have to babysit them."

Smith shook his head in disbelief. "You're not babysitting. Go to Moscow, find out where the threat comes from, and eliminate it."

"And win gold medals," Chiun said.

"Maybe they give one out for stupid assignments," Remo said. He looked at their faces and threw up his hands. "All right, all right. Pick an event. Not a marathon or anything like that. Something that doesn't take a lot of time. I just want to get in there and get out of there is all."

"We will let an impartial party decide what medal you should win," Chiun said. He stood up and walked to the sleeping drunk, touching him quickly on the shoulder. The man did not stir. Chiun called out twice, softly. "Wake up. Wake up." The man did not move. Chiun took the man's right earlobe between thumb and forefinger and squeezed.

"Yeow," the man yelled, jerking awake. He looked around in surprise, and saw Chiun standing in front of him, resplendent in a heavily brocaded yellow daytime robe.

"I must be dreaming," the derelict said. He rubbed his ear. But if he was dreaming, why did his ear hurt so much?

"Listen," said Chiun. "We are not concerned with your stupid ear. What kind of gold medal should we win in the Olympics?"

"You?" the drunk said. He looked Chiun over carefully. "Maybe the Golden Age Mile. You can all walk."

"Not me," Chiun said. "My student." He pointed and the man craned his neck to get a better look at Remo.

"He don't look so young either," the drunk said. "And he don't look like no athlete. I'm thirsty."

"Pick an event," Chiun insisted.

"Something that's not too hard. Maybe he can run. He looks like he's been running from cops. Can you run? A half-mile. Maybe he can run a half a mile?" He decided he was awake and he wondered who these people were and what they were doing in his zoo. Maybe while he was asleep someone had taken him from the zoo to the asylum.

"Yeah, I can run a half-mile," Remo said.

"Okay. Do a half-mile. Or meters. I think they do it in meters now. America has switched to the metric system. They even sell booze by liters now. And there's meters and millimeters and like that." He swelled his chest with pride. He felt like a patriot.

"Shut up," Chiun said. "Thank you." He returned to Remo. "Give the man a nickel for his trouble."

Remo walked over to the drunk, who was still mumbling about meters and millimeters and liters. Remo slipped a fifty-dollar bill into the derelict's hand, keeping his back turned so that Smith, who paid all the bills, would not see.

"Here," Remo said. "Buy yourself an imperial load on."

"I don't believe all this," Smith said.

"He will win," Chiun said. "You will see."

"I can't wait," Smith said.

The cable car bumped to a stop at the platform and the drunk scurried out of the car, running with his new-found fortune to the nearest bar and, in the process, setting his own lifetime best for the 983-yard run.

When Smith, Remo, and Chiun stepped from the car, they noticed that everyone else in the zoo seemed to be running too.

"Something's happened," Smith said.

"These people are scared," Remo said. A man in

40

a zoo guard's uniform ran toward them and Remo collared him.

"What's going on, pal?"

"Brian's escaped," the man said, as if that explained everything. He tried to resume running, but felt rooted to the spot. The skinny man's hand on his shoulder seemed to weigh a ton.

"That's great," Remo said. "Who's Brian?"

"Gorilla. Biggest gorilla in the world. Somebody got him riled and he snapped the cage door. He's going crazy. Lemme go. I gotta call for tranquilizer guns, buddy. Lemme go."

"Which way to the gorilla cage?" Chiun asked.

"Straight ahead," the guard said. "C'mon, lemme go."

Remo released the man's shoulder and the guard fled.

"We'd better leave," Smith said.

"Nonsense," said Chiun. "We will go to the gorilla. This will not really show you how fast Remo can run, but it may restore your faith in him, even if he is white, God help him, present company excepted. Come."

Chiun walked toward the cage. Smith looked at Remo, who shrugged and followed Chiun. And because he could think of no place safer, Smith walked after them.

When they reached the area of the gorilla cage, the zoo was practically empty, and Brian was calming down. If he could be kept there, away from the main walkways of the zoo, it should not be too difficult for zoo guards with tranquilizer guns to recapture him.

Chiun had other ideas.

"There he is," Smith hissed.

"It's all right," Remo said. "You can talk up. Gorillas don't know you're talking about them."

41

"Listen to Remo, Emperor. He knows about gorillas. And Monkeys."

Brian was seven feet tall and weighed more than 500 pounds. He was standing near his cage, scratching his head, looking around. When he saw the three men approaching, he jumped up and down, roared, and beat on his chest. Then he started toward them.

"We'd better leave here," Smith advised again.

"No need," said Chiun. "Remo will put the beast back in his cage."

"Why me?" Remo asked. "Why not you?"

"It is true," Chiun said, "that I have much more experience dealing with an ape, considering what I have had to endure in the last ten years, but I have no need to impress the emperor. You show him what you can do."

Remo sighed. Arguing with Chiun was a waste of time. It would be easier to put the damn gorilla back where he belonged.

"He's getting closer," Smith said. "I'd appreciate it if you fellows would agree on who was going to do what, or else let us get out of here."

"Easy does it, Smitty. Animals sense when you get nervous and it makes them mean," said Remo.

"I'll take your word for it," Smith said. "Let's go."

"The demonstration is set," Chiun said imperiously. He folded his arms and looked inscrutable.

"I'll put him back," Remo said.

"And do not hurt him," Chiun said. "He might be a relative."

The gorilla was almost on them now, so Remo took a large step forward, ducked inside the beast's swinging arms, put a hand on the massive hard chest and pushed.

Brian staggered back several feet, a look of cartoon surprise on his face. He did not understand what had happened and the noises this creature was making at him.

Smith didn't understand Remo's noises either.

"I am Everyman," Remo announced to Brian, "and I order you back to your cage."

"What is he talking about?" Smith asked Chiun.

"Merely talking to confuse the beast," Chiun answered, but he was frowning. Remo was playing games again. It was getting to be a habit and it could be a dangerous habit. Even gorillas could be dangerous if one's mind were not on one's work.

"Back," Remo ordered again but Brian lurched forward. Remo again ducked under the groping arms of the beast. He clamped his hand on the back of the gorilla's left thigh, found the muscle he wanted and squeezed. Brian fell to his knee, his left leg unable to hold his weight.

Using his left arm in place of a leg, Brian came forward again, grabbing for Remo with his right hand. Remo put up his own right hand and he and the gorilla clasped hands, making one fist of the two. Brian's hand dwarfed Remo's, but as Smith watched in disbelief, Remo began to exert pressure and the gorilla leaned backwards and finally dropped to both his knees.

"I don't believe this," Smith said. He looked anxiously around to see if anyone else was watching, but he saw no one. He was afraid that any moment now there would be news photographers and television crews and questions and interviews and the end of CURE, because that would be the result of going public.

"You must believe what you see," Chiun told Smith. But Smith did not hear him. He watched in wonder instead, as Remo picked up the 500-pound ape, tossed him over his shoulder, and carried him back to his cage. Remo gently lowered Brian to the floor of the cage, patted him on the head like a tame dog, and walked out. He left the door open behind

43

him but that did not matter. Brian had no more inclination to play.

"Satisfied?" Remo asked.

"Eminently," Smith said. "Let's go."

"I am not," said Chiun. "You took too long. You did not have to humiliate the poor beast." Chiun turned to Smith and bowed. "I apologize to you, O Emperor, for the sloppiness of the demonstration. He will improve."

"It's all right," Smith said.

"Are you sure?" Remo asked Smith. "You know, we could let a tiger out or something and try again."

"Let us just leave," Smith said.

"All right. Our car's just over there in that lot," Remo said.

"No car for you, meat-eater," Chiun said. "You are in training. You will run behind the vehicle."

As they strolled away, four guards with tranquilizer rifles ran up and stopped. Among them was the guard Remo had talked to earlier.

"Well, where's Brian?" one asked.

"He was here," the guard said. "I swear. Hey, Mac. You see the gorilla?"

"Sure," Remo said. "He's in his cage. But you better fix that door. He might get out."

CHAPTER FIVE

The seven runners on the luxurious, multimillion-dollar running track at Emerson College in Boston were wearing, among them, a total of $840 in running shoes with special air-lite paper-thin uppers and all-surface, all-weather Tiger-Paw spikes for better traction, and $700 of running clothes, including skin-tight shorts and tank-top shirts, aerodynamically designed to cut wind resistance in an amount that the manufacturer said might improve performance by as much as one tenth of one percent. In a mile race of 230 seconds, this could mean a faster speed of 23 hundredths of a second, and that might be the difference between so-so and a world's record.

And then there was Remo Black, the newcomer. Nobody had heard much about him, except that he had won pre-Olympic elimination races in Seattle, Portland, and Denver. He walked onto the track last. He was wearing black chinos and soft hand-made black Italian loafers. He wore a black cotton t-shirt with printing on the front. The shirt's legend read: I AM A VIRGIN.

Under that in much smaller type, the legend continued: "This is a very old t-shirt."

He had his wallet in his left rear pocket.

"He's got his wallet in his back pocket," said Vincent Josephs. "You see that? He's got his wallet in his back pocket. And the sucker's wearing chinos.

And loafers. This frigging hoople's wearing loafers. Is that what you brought me up here to see?"

He turned in his seat in the stands and looked through his Gucci semi-tint glasses with the wrap-around frames and the easy-ride earpiece at the man sitting next to him. Wally Mills was a track coach who had had three athletes competing in the preliminary Olympic trials in the 800-meter event. But as he had told his wife, "They couldn't beat me," and they had fallen by the wayside early. But he had seen Remo Black run twice, and so he had gotten hold of Vincent Josephs.

"That's part of his charm," Mills told Josephs. "I'm telling you this guy is not to be believed. Last week, in Portland, he ran away from the field like they was standing still. A new world's record, he coulda had. He was running like in a daze, and then, I swear to God to you, he slowed down and let them catch up and he just trotted along and finished second."

"So what? He ran out of gas," Josephs said.

Mills shook his head. "Like in horse racing, Mr. Josephs, he was full of run at the end. I had the glasses on him and he deliberately let everybody catch up. It was like he suddenly realized he was going to set a record and he didn't want to."

"All right," Josephs said. "So he's fast. That makes him a fast kook. Look at that t-shirt. That's like wearing a sail. And the guy's old. What's he doing with these kids? He's gonna have a frigging coronary. I'm just glad we ain't got him signed up by now."

"I swear to you, Mr. Josephs, this guy isn't even out of breath at the end of a race. He doesn't even walk around to catch his breath. These twenty-year-olds are all huffing and puffing and gasping and choking and he goes over and sits down and he looks

47

like he just woke up from a nap. So that's why I called you. I figured with you representing great athletes and all, this Remo Black might be a real dark horse for you."

Josephs was not convinced. "I'll watch him," he said. "Who's the chink?"

Mills said, "Korean, I think."

"What I said, a chink. Who's he?"

"He's this Remo's trainer or something. He's always around."

"A chink." Josephs shook his head in exasperation. "Mills, why are you wasting my frigging time on these people?"

"Watch him run," Mills said.

"I guess I got no choice," Josephs said, folding his arms and turning away. "But I think you ought to know that I got seven basketball contracts to negotiate and I'm working on a big deal for that dippy little gymnastic kid that everybody goes la-de-da about."

"But you ain't got a world champion," Mills said. "This guy could be one."

"Yeah, sure," Josephs said, but he decided to pay attention because Wally Mills was a good track coach and the truth was that the seven basketball players he represented, working together for a week, couldn't drop a basketball into an open manhole, and his deal for the little girl gymnast required him to figure out a way to make a pre-menstrual twelve-year-old look believable endorsing a special line of super-safe sanitary napkins, and the little broad was so dumb, it'd be another twelve years before she figured out what sanitary napkins were for.

Mills was right. He needed a world champion. A Mark Spitz. A Bruce Jenner. Somebody worth something, so he could package him right into that great golden tomorrow of cornflakes and mustache wax and men's clothes and you-name-it, all at a mere ten percent, sign here, kid, you'll never regret it.

He needed a world champion and hadn't been offered anything better than some middle-aged guy with chinos and an I-am-a-virgin t-shirt.

He would watch and see. They were all pieces of meat and maybe this piece of meat *could* run. If he finished in the top three and made the Olympic team, well, maybe, just maybe America was ready for a flake. What was the name of that guy who did the high jumping in the Donald Duck shirt? Everybody seemed to like him. Maybe this could be the same kind of find. Of course, he'd have to figure out a way to cut out Wally Mills and the chink, but if he waved enough promises under this Remo's nose, he shouldn't have any trouble getting him to come along.

To hell with it. The thing to do was to sit back and watch the race and see what happened.

Down on the field, Chiun was giving Remo his usual pre-race instructions.

"Remember, do not run too fast."

"I know, Chiun."

"Yes, I know you know, but it doesn't hurt to remind you. Last week, you almost set a world's record. That was dangerous. If I hadn't thrown that pebble at you to get your attention, who knows what foolishness you might have committed? Now, just run well enough to make the team. The Olympics. That is where world's records shall fall before us like grass before the honed blade."

"Yes, Little Father," Remo said. The truth was, and he didn't want to tell it to Chiun, that he was beginning to enjoy running fast. That was why he had gotten carried away the week before and almost run at high speed. It took a pebble thrown by Chiun, hitting him right behind the ear, to wake him up. But he had decided against telling Chiun that he was beginning to enjoy the competition because Chiun was suspicious of anything that Remo enjoyed doing.

49

Better to let him think that Remo was still doing this only from a sense of duty.

"Hey. Old man."

Remo did not turn around. He looked down at his loafers to make sure the soles didn't have holes in them because no matter how much money he paid for his hand-made Italian shoes, they weren't designed for running. Maybe when he went to the Olympics, he would buy a pair of sneakers. Maybe he would buy them before he went to Moscow. In Moscow, he had heard the shoe factories spent one year making size eights and the next year size nines and so on. This might be their year for making a size that wasn't Remo's and he might not be able to get sneakers. He would buy them before going to Moscow.

"Hey, old man," the voice came again. "You with the loafers."

Remo turned around to see a tall twenty-year-old with muscular legs, blond hair, and a mocking smile staring at him.

"What are you dressed up for, Pops? A masquerade party?"

"Are you talking to me?" Remo asked.

"Who else?"

"I thought you were talking to him," Remo said, nodding toward Chiun.

"He said 'old man'," Chiun said. "What does that have to do with me?"

"Never mind," Remo said. He turned back to the blond. "Just what is it you want?"

"What I want is to know what you think you're doing here running with us? You looking for a coronary? And who is this guy?" He looked at Chiun. "Hey, Fu Manchu. What is it you do?"

The blond began to laugh uproariously at his own rhymed wit. He trotted up and down in place, to keep his muscles warm. Chiun stepped over to him and placed one of his slippered feet on the young man's right foot.

He stopped trotting. It felt as if his foot had been instantly and totally nailed to the ground.

"Hey," he yelled. "Cut that out."

"Young bassoon," Chiun said, "your spirit is about to be broken. Remember this. No matter how fast you run, Remo here will always be one step ahead of you. One step. You will never to be able to pass him, no matter how hard you try, no matter how fast you run. This is a promise the Master of Sinanju makes to you for your insolence."

Chiun stepped off the blond's foot and the man stared at him, confused, wondering how somebody so small could weigh so much when he stepped on a foot.

"Don't worry," the blond said. "Your guy's going to eat my dust."

"Always one step behind, loudmouth," Chiun reminded him, holding up one finger topped with a long curved nail.

When he stepped back to Remo, he was asked, "Why didn't you just smack him in the mouth, Chiun?"

"I would have," Chiun said, "but I don't know the stupid rules for this stupid race. Maybe if this clod doesn't run, there are not enough people or something and we would have to do this all over. I thought it better to do what I did."

"Well, I don't mind you making promises that I have to keep, Chiun, but I think you'd better hope for one thing."

"Which is?"

"That this blond lump runs at least fourth. 'Cause if you want me to stay just one step in front of him and he's at the back of the pack, I'm out of the Olympics. There goes all your endorsement money, not to mention Smitty getting sore."

51

Chiun waved his hand airily. "You just make sure he doesn't run worse than fourth place. It will give you something to do. Now, get over there with the others because I don't think they will let you start the race from a sitting position here on the bench."

The seven other runners took their places in the starting block. Remo just stood up in lane five, his hands in his pockets, waiting for the gun. The blond was in lane three and Remo decided that as soon as the gun sounded, he would hook up with the guy and keep one step ahead of him all the way. He'd worry about the end of the race when he got to it.

The gun crackled in the thin Boston air and the runners sprinted off. Remo moved up alongside the blond, then moved one step ahead of him. They were running fifth and sixth, while one of the runners cut a blistering pace in first place. The race was two laps around the track and a little extra, and halfway through the first lap, the blond grunted to Remo, "Let's see how good you are, Gramps." He increased his speed, intending to zip by Remo, but Remo kept one step ahead of him, running easily. He felt cinders off the track kick up against his chinoed legs and the breeze in his face was cool and sweet. He liked running, he decided.

As they finished the first lap, the pacesetter began to tire. Remo and his blond shadow moved up and were now running third and fourth. They held that position until they were halfway around the track in the final lap. The blond grunted again, "Time to let it all hang out. See you, Pops."

He went into a kick, lengthened his stride and stepped up the speed of his step. Remo responded by finally taking his hands out of his pockets, and the blond saw Remo, still there, still one step ahead of him. He pushed harder but he could not make up that one step. Two runners passed them. Remo could hear the blond's breath begin to come in short, sharp little bursts.

Now what would he do if this bumpkin quit cold on him? They were coming around the final turn now for the backstretch. Remo closed the few inches that separated them and clamped his right hand on the blond man's left wrist, then began to run faster, pulling the other man with him. They had faded to fifth and sixth and Remo, with the blond now in tow, stepped up his speed. As they neared the finish line, he kicked in the afterburners, moving up into third place and towing the collapsing blond along into fourth. As they crossed the line, Remo let go of the younger man's wrist and the blond, who had not controlled his own forward motions for the last 100 yards, went sprawling forward on his face, tumbling forward, rolling over until he came to a stop. He lay there, unable to move, trying to catch his breath. His legs felt leaden; his lungs sucked acid and exhaled fire.

He saw Remo standing over him, no expression on his sharply angled face, not breathing hard, not even sweating.

He closed his eyes to blot out the sight of Remo's face, but he heard Remo's voice say: "Nice race, junior. I guess I'm just one step better than you."

Remo strolled back to the bench on the infield where he found Chiun frowning at him.

"What's wrong now? I did what you said, didn't I?"

"Yes, but you did not win."

"I had something else on my mind. Besides, I only had to finish third to get to Moscow. You said save the good stuff for the Games."

"But I didn't tell you to embarrass me."

Remo started to answer, then thought better of it. Chiun would have his say, no matter what.

53

"You will have to redeem me in Moscow," Chiun said. "There you can make me look like the greatest of all trainers. I will be approached to reveal my great secrets for making a lump like you into a runner. They will ask me to do television guest shots and I will make much money for my village. Maybe I will even get my own show."

"Heeeeeeeeeeeere's Chiun," said Remo.

Chiun did not smile. "All this will happen in Moscow where you will atone for shaming me today."

Remo bowed gravely and said: "As you wish, Little Father."

Up in the stands, Vincent Josephs was not pleased.

"That's your super runner?" he asked Mills. "He was never in the race."

Wally Mills thought for a moment before replying. Should he tell Josephs what he thought he saw? That this Remo was busy pulling that other runner across the finish line? No. He couldn't tell him that. It was so unbelievable, he wasn't sure he believed it himself. Instead he said, "You're mistaken, Mr. Josephs. He was where he wanted to be every step of the way. He wasn't even trying for some reason, but he made sure to qualify. Did you see him close?"

Josephs conceded to himself that Mills had a point. The guy did close fast to get up for third place. Of course, the blond guy closed fast too, but he was a loser, so ignore him. Well, why not? It wouldn't do any harm to go down and talk to this Remo, convince him to sign in advance of the Olympics just in case he did win something in Russia.

"Maybe I'll go down and talk to him, just so this trip won't be a total waste of time," Josephs said.

"I'll go with you," Mills said.

They made their way down to the field, hoping to catch Remo before he left.

"Hey, pal," Josephs called. "You with the t-shirt."

Remo turned, saw Josephs, and did not like what

he saw. He saw a big cigar, a couple of flashy rings, tinted eyeglasses, a well-tailored three-piece suit that couldn't hide a fat, soft body, and a loud mouth.

"What do you want?"

"You run pretty good, pal," Josephs said. "My name's Vincent Josephs. You hear of me?"

"No," Remo said.

Josephs frowned. Well, it didn't matter. Someday the whole world would have heard of him.

"Listen, buddy, you and me might be able to make some money. Together, you know. Endorsements and things. I mean, you run pretty good in those dungarees and—"

"Chinos," Remo said. "I don't wear dungarees."

"Yeah, chinos. And loafers. Maybe you could run really fast if you wore shorts and running shoes."

"Can't," Remo told him, as he turned and walked away with Chiun. He heard the pest padding up heavily behind him.

"Why can't you?" Josephs asked him.

"It's against my beliefs to flaunt my flesh."

"Huh?"

"Nothing. Forget it. Look, I don't need a promoter or an agent, thank you."

"Excuse me, what's your name, Remo, but you're wrong. You need me to make a bundle."

Chiun stopped and turned and so did Remo. Chiun shook his head. "All he needs is me," he said.

"You?" Josephs laughed and turned back to Remo. "You and me together, kid, we can do it. I'll package you and—"

"If you don't get out of here, I'll package you," Remo said.

"Calm down, kid," Josephs said, gesturing with his hands. "If you want to keep the old fella, keep him. He can do your laundry or something."

"You know, you talk too much," Remo said. He asked Chiun, "Don't you think he talks too much?"

"Not anymore," Chiun said. Neither Josephs nor Mills sat Chiun's hand move. Only Remo's eyes could follow the motion. But suddenly Josephs felt a great pressure on his throat.

Josephs opened his mouth to cry out but no sound would come. His eyes bulged as he tried to speak but he could make no sound.

"What—what happened?" asked Mills.

"I paralyzed his vocal cords. His chatter was beginning to offend me," Chiun said.

Josephs was clutching at his throat, trying to force sound, any kind of sound, but nothing came out.

"Will he stay that way?" Mills asked.

Chiun answered blandly, "It depends on how much damage I did. I only meant it to be a temporary silencing, but his constant noise might have thrown my concentration off."

Remo shook his head at Mills. Nothing could disturb Chiun's concentration. "Temporary," Remo said. "Just temporary. Take him somewhere and tell him to relax. He'll be shooting off his mouth again in no time."

"All right, Mr. Black," said Mills. "I'll do that." He took Josephs by the elbow and led him away. Josephs still held his throat.

"I think we should go back to the hotel and let the emperor know you were semi-successful today even if you did disgrace me," Chiun said.

"You go tell him that if you want," Remo said. "I'm going to hang around and watch some of the other athletes for a while."

"Very well. But remember curfew," Chiun said.

"Yes, Little Trainer," said Remo.

CHAPTER SIX

In an arena filled with female gymnasts, anyone with a bosom would have been a standout, but the woman Remo was watching would have stood out in any company. She was in her early twenties and stood five-foot-five and weighed 120 pounds. This made her bigger, heavier and older than any other female competitor in the gym. And more beautiful. Her dark brown hair would have fallen to mid-back if it had not been tied up in a bun, her chin was square, and her cheekbones high. Her lips were full and her teeth even and white against the light coppery tan of her skin. Her eyes, he saw when she turned her head his way, were a soft, wet brown. She had the exquisitely shaped legs of a gymnast without the bulging lumpy muscle mass.

Remo saw her as he strolled around the gymnasium and he stopped to watch. Even as he did, he reflected that this was curious behavior on his part. Among the lessons that Chiun had taught him as part of the wisdom of Sinanju had been a series of twenty-six steps for lovemaking, twenty-six steps to bring a woman to indescribable ecstasy. Remo had rarely found a woman who could go past thirteen and generally he didn't care. When the risk of failing at sex had been taken out of it, the fun went too. And so, seemingly, did the urge. Until this young woman. Remo wanted to meet her. There was something about her.

He was impressed, too, when he watched her perform on the balance beam, the four-inch-wide piece of wood on which women did ballet and acrobatics. Her size was a disadvantage she would have to overcome, but she was good and Remo saw the potential for more than just good. She could be trained.

She finished her routine on the beam with a twisting somersault dismount, grabbed a towel and ran to the edge of the gym floor, where she stood anxiously looking toward the scorers' table. Remo stepped alongside her.

"You were good," he said.

She looked around, surprised at his voice, then smiled perfunctorily, and looked back toward the table.

"Really good," he said.

"I hope the judges think so."

"What do you need to qualify?"

"Nine-point-three," she said.

They watched and waited until the judges posted her score. They gave her a nine-point-four. She squealed with joy as she jumped into the air. Remo was the closest person to her so she threw her arms around him and hugged him. He felt her firm breasts press against his chest and smelled the sweet cut-grass scent of her hair.

"Oh," she said, suddenly recoiling, realizing she was hugging a stranger. She put her hands over her mouth, then lowered them. "I'm sorry," she said.

"I'm not," Remo said. "Congratulations."

"Thank you. Are you competing?"

Remo nodded. "Eight hundred meters. I qualified, too."

"Congratulations back. What's your name?"

"Remo Black. Yours?"

"Josie Littlefeather," she answered, watching him closely for a reaction.

"Pretty," was all he said.

"Thanks. And thanks for not making some smart-ass remark."

"One wasn't called for," Remo said. "Listen, since we're both celebrating, why don't we do it together? I'll spring for a drink."

"Make it coffee and it's a go," she said.

She walked to a nearby bench and shared hugs with a half dozen other gymnasts, all of them smaller and younger than Josie was. She put on a wrap-around skirt and slid her feet into a pair of sandals and was ready to go. She looked more like the average girl on Main Street than an Olympic athlete, Remo thought, and then decided that with his t-shirt, chinos and loafers, he looked like an outboard motor mechanic.

As they walked from the gym, Josie wrapped a silk handkerchief around her neck.

"I could use a shower," she said.

"So could I, but coffee first. I've got a curfew."

"Don't we all?" the woman said.

She had wanted coffee, but with every step they took away from the mammoth Emerson College Fieldhouse, the thought of food penetrated deeper and deeper into her mind.

"Food," Josie said. "I want food. Swooping large amounts of food, piled on my plate."

"A carbohydrate junkie," Remo said.

"Yeah. Everybody I know, after an event, it's roll out the pasta. Well, you know how it is."

"Sure," lied Remo, who had heard about carbohydrate depletion but knew nothing about it since his diet was largely restricted to rice and fish and occasional fresh vegetables and fruit, all Chiun's Korean food staples and all so damned tasteless that Remo truly didn't care if he ate or starved.

They found a Szechuan restaurant two blocks away from the college and Josie Littlefeather insisted that she wanted Chinese food. As they walked inside, the pungent odors flooded Remo's nostrils and he remembered with a touch of hurt that he was never again going to eat noodles with cold sesame paste or spicy-hot General Chien's chicken, or sliced giant prawns in smooth red garlic sauce. However, he made sure he ordered all of them for Josie Littlefeather and he sipped at water as he watched her eat like a gleeful satisfied animal and he recognized that she ate as she performed on the beam—with joy. And Remo realized also that he found very little joy in his life since learning the secrets of Sinanju. There was no joy in sex and no joy in food and there was never any joy in killing because it was both art and science and its purity was its own reward. In making him more of a man, had Sinanju made him somehow less of a human? He wondered. And he wondered, too, if it had all been worth it.

Josie started off eating with chopsticks which she maneuvered well, but found incapable of holding at one jab the amount of food she wanted to stuff into her face, so she resorted to a soupspoon.

"We're going to swap life stories, Remo Black," she said, "but my mouth is going to be full so tell me yours first."

Remo did. He made it all up. He invented a family and a hometown and a past and told her that he had always wanted to complete in the Olympics but it wasn't until he had hit the state lottery of ten thousand dollars that he was able to quit his job in the auto junkyard and go into training.

"Sure, I'm older than the rest of the runners, but I don't think that's going to stop me from making a good showing," he said.

"I admire you," she told him, chewing unabashedly. "You know what you want and you're not letting anything stop you from trying to get it." Which Remo knew was a crock because what he wanted was to yank the bowl of noodles with sesame

61

paste away from her and drop it into his mouth in one large sticky lump, and he was letting just the memory of Chiun's training stop him from doing that.

He contented himself with, "How about you? Do you know what you want?"

She nodded. "I'm an Indian. I want to give my people something to be proud of."

"What tribe?"

"Blackhand. A reservation in Arizona." She looked upward toward the ceiling as if her life's memories were written on the grease-saturated Celotex. "You know what it's like. People who are—well, limp. Even the children. Once warriors. Now they make a living selling junk blankets and doing phony rain dances for tourists. I can't change that, but maybe I can give them something to hang their pride on." She looked at Remo with an almost-electric intensity. "I want that gold medal. For my people."

Remo felt something close to shame. Here was a woman—not a girl like most of the other competitors but a woman—who had spent God knows how many years trying to get to the Olympics, and to him it had all been a piece of cake. Winning a gold metal would be no more difficult for Remo than walking across an empty street.

At that moment, he made up his mind to help Josie Littlefeather win a gold medal for her people. And for herself.

She was talking to him. "And why do you want a gold medal, Remo?"

He shook his head. "It's not important, Josie. Not half as important, or noble, as why you want it."

Her laugh lit her face. Her eyes twinkled and she nodded her head in a mock curtsey. "Is that what I am? Noble?"

"Noble and beautiful and I'm going to help you get that medal," he said. He took her hands in his and squeezed them. He did not recognize these emotions. He had not felt this way in years, perhaps too many years, and he didn't want to think about the other women who had made him feel that way before because they were all dead. They were monuments to Remo's life and work. And they were all dead.

"Are you entered in anything else?" Remo asked.

"Yes. The overall. But balance beam is my best. Have you ever been on a balance beam, Remo?"

"Surely you jest," Remo said. "I was born on one. And when I'm through with you, watch out, world. Nothing but tens."

She squeezed his hands back. "Heavy promise, white man."

"If I lie, you can hang me on your belt. Look. That fieldhouse must be empty by now. After all, you've been eating non-stop for six hours. Let's go back there and take a look at that balance beam of yours."

She nodded. "After this buildup, you'd better not disappoint me and fall off the damn thing."

If Josie Littlefeather had been a judge, watching Remo's performance on the beam, her only complaint would have been that she could not give a score higher than ten.

Remo had kicked off his Italian loafers, hopped up onto the beam in the empty gymnasium, and done work she had never seen before, not even in her dreams. He executed front flips, back flips, double fronts, and double backs. He moved so swiftly and surely that sometimes there appeared to be more than one Remo on the beam. He finished with a dismount she had never even seen attempted before, a two-and-a-half somersault. And Remo did it from a one-hand hand stand. He finished with his feet together on the mat and raised his arms to eleven

63

o'clock and one o'clock, the way he had seen gymnasts do on television.

He looked at her for approval and she applauded.

"Tens?" she said. "Hell. Thirteens. Twenties. You're a perfect twenty, man." She ran over and hugged him, but it was a different hug from the one she had given him earlier by mistake. This time he put his arms around her and hugged her back. Then he kissed her and for a moment her mouth was soft and yielding, but suddenly she stiffened and pushed away from him. He did not loosen his grip but instead held her at arm's length.

"I'm sorry," she told him haltingly. "I guess I'm just not very experienced."

"My fault," he said, letting his hands drop. "I shouldn't have done that." He did not like the way he felt. He was like a schoolboy with a crush. He turned back to the beam to mask the confusion on his face. "Why don't you do a routine for me and let me watch?"

"After what you just did? I'd feel like a cluck."

"Lesson number one," Remo said. "Don't think about anything except what *you're* doing. What were you thinking about when you did your last routine today?"

She looked sheepish. "I was thinking I needed a nine-three to qualify."

"Right. And that's why you almost didn't get it. From now on, you think about now. You don't even think two seconds ahead when you're on the beam." Even as he said it, he knew it was a lie and the wrong advice. He was trying to give her the art of Sinanju which required such a deep ingraining of technique that technique was never thought of consciously. One didn't think at all. Physical things were best when they flowed instinctively from one's body without thought. That was Sinanju and Chiun had given it to him, but it had taken more than ten laborious years. Remo could make Josie Littlefeather the best balance beam artist in the world, but he could not give her Sinanju, not in time for the Olympics. But he vowed to try.

As she walked toward the beam, a voice bellowed through the gymnasium, echoing off the walls and quonset-curved roof.

"Well, well," the voice said and Remo turned to the door. It was the blond runner, the one who had promised to feed Remo dust and had wound up being pulled across the finish line. He seemed to have recovered both his wind and his sneer.

"What's this, Pops?" he asked Remo. "Getting into girls' activities now? Or just trying to get into the girl?"

"I never got your name," Remo said.

"My name? Chuck Masters. The guy you screwed and the guy who's going to kick your ass back to wherever you came from."

"What good's that going to do you?" Remo asked.

"I break you up some and you have to pull out of the games. As next finisher, I move up into your spot and go to Moscow. We can do it my way or you can just volunteer to drop out. What do you say?"

He looked at Remo with his hands raised in a questioning gesture, a small nasty smile on his mouth.

"Go stick a javelin in your ear," Remo said. He turned back to Josie and Masters called, "Don't turn your back on me. And you, Littlefeather, what are you doing hanging out with him?"

"None of your business," she said.

Remo wondered how they knew each other and how well. He liked Chuck Masters even less now. He turned back in time to see Masters hoisting up to his chest a weightlifter's barbell, loaded with 150 pounds.

"Strong, but no brains," Remo told Josie. She laughed.

Masters pushed the barbells at Remo. Josie's sharp intake of breath echoed in the hushed gymnasium. Remo bent slightly and with a flick of a wrist, assisted the weights in sailing over his head. The barbell hit on the floor with a jangling crash.

"Bad throw, big mouth," said Remo. Masters's face reddened. He yanked up another weight, this one loaded at 200 pounds. He got it to his chest and began to walk toward Remo.

"Chuck, stop it," Josie shouted. "Stop it."

"Here. Try this one on for size," Masters said.

Remo said to Josie, "No brains. He even talks like a comic book."

Remo turned back in time to watch the 200 pounds of weight leave Masters's hand and sail through the air toward him. He smiled slightly as he reached out his right hand and caught the barbell with it and held it there, straight out in front of him with one hand.

Masters's eyes goggled.

"What the—"

"My turn, bigmouth. I'll pitch, you catch."

"Now, listen—" Masters started but it was too late. To him it looked as if Remo had simply opened his hand but the barbell was coming back at him. Fast. He snapped his hands up to his chest to protect himself. Masters caught the barbell awkwardly in both hands but the force of Remo's toss pushed him back and down and as he hit the floor, the barbell slipped out of his hands and off his chest and rolled upward so that it straddled his neck, pressing lightly on his Adam's apple.

"Take this off me," Masters pleaded. But instead, Remo stepped up onto the bar, his feet on either side of Masters's chin. The slight pressure of his weight bent the center of the bar slightly and it bellied down even more against Masters's throat. The blond man screamed.

"Do yourself a favor," Remo said coldly. "Don't ever come near us again." He felt himself almost shiver with anger and quickly he turned back toward Josie.

"Curfew," he told her. "We'd better go."

"What about him?" she asked. There was fright in her eyes as she looked at Remo, as if she were seeing him for the first time.

"Leave him. He'll get it off when he stops panicking. Don't worry about him."

He led her to the gymnasium door. At the exit, she looked back at Masters, but Remo pulled her outside. They walked to her hotel in Copley Square without saying a word to each other. Remo knew what was wrong. He had changed during those few moments with Chuck Masters, and Josie had caught a glimpse of a different Remo and she was confused and perhaps frightened. Remo did not try to speak to her. He didn't know how he could tell her that it was only her presence that had kept Masters alive to pester someone else another day. He simply left the Indian girl at her door and told her he would see her in Moscow. And continue her balance beam lessons.

Chiun was waiting for Remo when he got back to his own room. He was pacing the floor.

"Where were you?" he demanded.

"I broke training," Remo said.

"So. This is how it starts. Five minutes late now. Ten minutes tomorrow. Soon you will be staying out to all hours of the night, coming home looking like something the cat does doo-doo in, and there goes my gold medal."

"*Your* gold medal?"

"Yes," Chiun said, without acknowledging Remo's sarcasm. "My gold medal. My endorsements. My fame. The security for my old age."

"Get off my case," Remo said. "That creep from the race, that blond guy, pestered me."

"And what did you do?"

"I just played with him a little."

"You did well. I do not know if I could have been that lenient with him. There was a time when you would not be so lenient either."

Remo realized that Chiun missed nothing.

"Is there something you wish to tell me?" Chiun asked.

"No, Little Father, I just want to sleep."

"As you wish. Emperor Smith is pleased. Arrangements are being made for Moscow. Go to sleep. Athletes, even those blessed with brilliant trainers, need to rest."

"Good night," Remo said. He went to bed, thinking that in Moscow, he would tell Chiun about Josie Littlefeather, who had made this assignment for Remo a very important, very personal matter.

CHAPTER SEVEN

Fires crackled in big holes dug into the sandy shore. Droplets of flame splashed into the night air as fat from the pigs turning on spits over the fires spattered down into the pits, caught aflame and flared upward.

Drums and bamboo flutes inserted sensuous melodies into the night and a dozen girls in tight, one-piece wraps danced back and forth across the white sand, plying large circles around three men who sat on the sand on tufted mats, watching the women with appreciation.

The biggest of the three men was Sammy Wanenko, who, along with the other two athletes, would represent his South Pacific island country of Baruba in the Moscow Olympic Games.

The hour neared midnight and soon the king of Baruba would select the three winners in the dancing competition. The three chosen women would spend the night with the three Olympic-bound athletes.

The island-country's custom was that all women of child-bearing age, whether married or not, must compete in the dance competition, and the hundreds of women had been narrowed down to these twelve finalists. The custom had just been invented, since this was Baruba's first Olympics, the country only recently having been accepted into the United Nations.

Baruba's membership had come after a week of debate. The non-aligned bloc in the UN demanded that Baruba change its name to the People's Democratic Republic of Baruba, which the king agreed to after being assured that the name had nothing to do with democracy, but was merely a way for Communist dictatorships to recognize each other.

The second requirement for membership was that the king of Baruba had to issue a statement, which would be written for him, attacking the United States for its colonial, imperialistic, warmongering policies toward the Baruban people. The king had no trouble with this since he had never met an American, had only the vaguest idea where America was, and had been cautioned that if he didn't, the United States might sneak into his country some night and steal all the pineapples.

The third requirement for UN membership was that the delegate to the United Nations refrain from showing up at the sessions of that international body with a bone in his nose. The foreign minister was reluctant to agree to this because he felt undressed without a bone in his nose, but he was mollified when the king promised him that he could wear a shell necklace instead and it would be the biggest shell necklace that anyone in Baruba had ever worn including the king.

There was a fourth potential requirement but it was voted down by the United Nations general assembly as racist, imperialist, Zionist-stoogeist and war-mongerist. This was the tart suggestion of the British delegate that the Barubans stop eating each other.

So on a warm Tuesday, the Peoples' Democratic Republic of Baruba was admitted to the United Nations. On Wednesday, its UN representative made a speech, written for him by the Russians, attacking the United States as racist. On Thursday, Baruba filed a request—written by the Russians—with Washington, asking for reparations for psychological damage suffered by the Barubans because of the imperialist Vietnam war. And on Friday night, they held a dancing contest to see which three women would sleep with the three Olympic-bound athletes.

The three athletes enjoyed watching the dancing girls and Sammy Wanenko particularly liked watching a young girl named Lonie who was married to an older man who had been unable to compete for the honor of going to the Olympics because of his age. Baruba's king had decided the country would send only its very best athletes. He set the cutoff age for competition at twenty-one, which he said was the prime of life. The king was twenty-one.

Lonie had been casting longing eyes at Sammy for the last six months, every time their paths crossed on the small island. She was seventeen and ripe but Sammy had stayed away from her, respecting her status as a married woman. But now, he knew that when she won the dancing competition she would be his.

An hour later, the king presented her to Sammy for the night. Eyes downcast in shyness, she was about to walk off with the athlete when a voice rang out from the fringes of the smiling crowd.

"No!"

Hundreds of heads turned, their smiles instantly frozen on their faces. A large man with muscled sloping shoulders, large rippling arms, and short powerful bull-like legs stepped out of the darkness at the edge of the crowd, where the pit fires had begun to burn down.

"It is Polo," someone hissed.

"Lonie's husband," said another. "This means trouble."

Polo pushed his way roughly through the crowd to the king's throne chair. He was twenty-seven years old.

"I will not allow it," Polo shouted. "If this Wanenko child wishes to sleep with my Lonie, he

72

will have to defeat me. I will show you he is not the greatest athlete in Baruba. That honor belongs to me." He turned and stared at Sammy, only feet away from the feather-robed king. Lonie shrank away from the two men. Polo sneered at Sammy. "Let this pup defeat me. Then you may call him the greatest."

Sammy looked at Polo, then the king. He found that the king was looking at him quizzically. Sammy turned and saw Lonie watching him. He saw her flashing eyes, her ripe young breasts, her full mouth, and he knew he wanted to have her, almost as much as he wanted to go to the Olympics.

He turned back to Polo. "I agree," he said.

The king looked up at Polo and said "What sport . . ." but before he could finish, Polo lashed out with a thundering right hand that caught Sammy high on the cheek. With a laugh, Polo shouted, "Brawling is my sport."

The blow knocked Sammy off balance and sprawling. Polo moved after him, swinging wildly, trying to finish the younger man early. But Sammy ducked and the blows went over his head. He straightened up from his crouch and pushed a short left into Polo's stomach, ridged hard with muscle. It drove some wind from the bigger man.

Both men regained their balance and turned to face each other again, moving about, feinting, trying to grab the feel of the other's movements. Sammy waited until the older man made his move.

As he had guessed, Polo had muscle but no speed. When he threw a right at Sammy, the younger man moved his head aside and scored with a left to Polo's nose. And again. And again. Polo's nose turned red and began to bleed.

The blood trickling down his face seemed to anger him and he charged Sammy and wrapped his muscular arms around him, pinning Wanenko's own arms to his side. Sammy felt the backward pressure. It seemed as if his spine would snap. Polo increased the pressure and Sammy, clearing his head, suddenly stopped trying to fight the strength in those massive arms and instead brought his knee up into Polo's crotch. The older man let out a scream of pain and Sammy broke free. Once he did, the young champion hacked three consecutive lefts into Polo's face, each one snapping the man's head back until, after the third blow, Polo fell to the ground and lay still.

The crowd cheered the young champion. So did Lonie, who could not wait to feel him on her body.

The king motioned to Sammy and Lonie that they might leave. The feast was over.

Polo was left lying in the sand while the three athletes went off to their homes with the three young women. As Sammy lay down with Lonie, she asked with a laugh, "Why did you not use your right hand? You defeated Polo with only one hand."

Sammy laughed. "I did not want to damage my right hand. I will need it to win my gold medal. In boxing."

Lonie turned away from him in mock anger. "For a mere gold medal you will use two hands. But poor Lonie, she is only worth one hand."

"No," Sammy said. "Two hands and two arms and two legs and this and this and this . . ."

Flight Lieutenant Jack Mullin searched the sky for the airplane. *It should be arriving soon,* he thought. He turned and looked at the other four men with him. They were beginning to get restless, anxious for some action, and this pleased Mullin. He had drilled them long and hard and they were his four best. Everything should go perfectly.

The four light-skinned blacks also scanned the sky, searching for the plane, occasionally glancing at the British mercenary to see if he, too, was showing any signs of nervousness.

74

Mullin smiled to himself as he thought how odd it was that his life had brought him here. In his life, he had had three loves and one great hate. He hated blacks and the thought almost made him laugh, because here he was, being paid by Jimbobwu Mkombu, the blackness of whose skin was matched only by the blackness of his heart. But Mkombu's money was very green and that was one of Mullin's three loves. Money, whisky and women. Right now, he had money in his pocket and fine Irish whisky in his canteen, so he thought back to the last woman he'd had. The African women in Mkombu's compound were all enthusiasm but no technique, willing to do anything Mullin wanted, but still poor replacement for an Irish lass. Or, for that matter, an Englishwoman.

The woman he was remembering was a red-haired, green-eyed woman with the biggest . . .

There it was.

His ears picked up the approaching plane even before he saw it. He got to his feet and called out: "Get ready, lads."

The four blacks got to their feet and held their breath to hear the plane. They soon spotted it, a tiny, faraway speck coming toward them, glinting golden in the sky where the morning sun reflected off it.

The first step in the slaughter of America's Olympic athletes was about to be taken.

Sammy Wanenko sat aboard the rented airplane, smiling. He had never had a night like that before and now he was ready for the Olympics. He was ready for any boxer the Russians or the Americans or the Cubans could send against him. He was ready for anyone or anything.

The plane had been rented, because Baruba did not have an air force or even an airplane, preferring until that very week to regard airplanes as manifesta-

75

tions of the great island god Lotto. This had changed when a plane had arrived on the island to take the UN ambassador to New York. The ambassador, still miffed at having to give up the bone in his nose, was reluctant to get on the plane. He pleaded with the king to let him swim to New York. Finally, the king forced him aboard, the plane took off, and the air age had reached the People's Democratic Republic of Baruba.

For their athletes, they rented the plane and the services of an Australian pilot, Johnny Winters. Winters was in his mid-thirties, unmarried, and for the past ten years had eked out a living transporting cargo and/or people, legal or illegal, for whoever would pay the freight.

His assignment was to fly the Baruban team to Melbourne, Australia, where they would board the jetliner that would take them to Moscow. His takeoff had been delayed that morning as he waited for his young co-pilot, Bart Sands. Sands was twenty-two, married, and with a second child on the way. He had been trying to make enough money on the horses to pay all the hospital bills and as a result, he was into both the bookies and the loan sharks.

Sands had been with Winters for about a year and had not learned a thing. He had managed to bail out from under his debts once, with a huge score at the track. But he just ignored Winters when the older man told him that lightning very rarely struck at all, let alone twice, and he should quit gambling.

Sands ignored the advice. When he arrived at the plane, Winters said, "I thought I was going to have to leave you behind. What happened? You have to get in a bet on a hot horse?"

"Something like that," Sands said. "C'mon, let's get this crate off the ground." There was a look on his generally smiling face that jarred Winters. There was something wrong. He didn't know what it was.

76

Sands hoped that Winters had not noticed anything strange about him. He also hoped that Winters didn't notice the bulge the .45 automatic was making under Sands's jacket.

Soon, he thought. *Soon all my money problems will be over and then I'll square it up with him. He'll understand it was the only way.*

The DC-3 landed on the beach at Baruba and Sammy Wanenko came aboard, along with the other two athletes, brothers named Tonny and Tomas and their coach, Willem. They waved from the windows of the plane until they were airborne. *At last,* Sammy thought, *I am on my way to win my gold medal.*

After they were in the air for half an hour, Bart Sands knew it was time.

Think about your pregnant wife, he told himself. *Think about what they said they'll do to Janie if you don't pay up. And the kids. It's quick money,* he told himself. *Quick money. That's all it is, with no one getting hurt.*

He took the .45 from under his jacket and pointed it at his friend, Johnny Winters.

Winters couldn't believe what he saw, but then he realized why the strained look had been on his friend's face when he had boarded the plane.

"Bart . . ." he began to say.

"Please, Johnny, don't," Sands said. "I promise you. No one will get hurt. This is the only way. And I promise, we'll split right down the middle."

Sands was talking too fast. Winters had never seen him this nervous. His hand was shaking uncontrollably. Winters hoped that he could just keep the kid from killing somebody by accident.

Willem, the Baruban coach, chose that moment to come up to the cockpit. He saw the gun and asked, "What is wrong, please?"

77

Sands got up from his seat, pushed Willem back into the passenger cabin, and waved the .45 at the four Barubans.

"Don't any of you move if you don't want to die," he said. Sammy Wanenko looked up into the barrel of the .45. He thought the man looked very nervous. Before he could think anymore, Willem, the coach, leaped from his seat at Sands.

Sammy saw the gun in the white man's hand jump. He saw Willem fall, clutching his stomach.

Sands could not speak for a moment. He was as surprised as anyone else when the gun in his hand went off. Could it possibly be that easy to kill a man?

Finally he found his voice. He told the three Barubans, "The same for you, if any of you move." He went back into the cockpit and told Winters: "Now you do what I say, if you want to live."

Winters realized the younger man suddenly sounded much more confident. He glanced over his shoulder and saw, with fright, that Bart Sands's gun hand had stopped shaking.

Sands recited from memory a new set of coordinates which would take them just slightly off their present course and Winters was puzzled. He knew the charts for this area of the Pacific by heart.

"Bart, there's nothing there. What are we doing?"

"Just do it, Johnny," said Sands. He felt sweat pouring from under his arms, but he was as surprised as Winters to find that his gun hand no longer shook.

Winters changed the direction of the plane. He knew of no island that corresponded with the location given him by Bart Sands.

Jack Mullin did.

He had intentionally chosen the island because it did not appear on any existing commercial charts. And rather than trust to luck to find an accomplice like Bart Sands, he had, through an intermediary, advanced the pilot more gambling money for more losses, and then had made him a proposition that would pay off all his debts and give him a nest egg besides.

Winters saw the uncharted island at the same time Bart Sands did.

"Land it there," Sands said. "On that stretch of beach."

The beach had been smoothed out and almost looked like a runway, Winters realized. Somebody had been there and somebody was expecting them. But who?

He nosed the plane down, and even though the wheels bit deeper into the wet sand than he expected, rolled it to a smooth stop.

"Get in the back with them," Sands said, waving his gun toward the Barubans in the back.

When Winters was seated, Sands warned them all to stay put. Then he opened the door between the cockpit and passenger cabin and climbed out.

There was a single shot.

Sammy Wanenko jumped to his feet and Winters, looking at Willem's body still sprawled in the aisle of the cabin, said "Take it easy, fella. We don't know what's out there."

"It does not matter," Sammy said. "I am not afraid."

"Maybe we all ought to be," Winters said.

Wanenko threw him a look of scorn but sat back in his seat.

Bart Sands, Winters knew, was dead. Of that he had no doubt. His payoff had been something less than he had expected, even less than he deserved.

What now?

* * *

79

The shot was a clean one, entering the back of Sands's head and tearing away most of his face as it exited.

Paid in full, thought Lieutenant Jack Mullin, as he holstered his .45.

He walked to the body, which was lying face down on the beach, tipped his hat to it in thanks and then walked to the plane. His four men followed, spread out in a fan shape behind him.

Mullin used the butt of his .45 to bang on the side of the plane.

"You lads can come out now," he called. When there was no reply from within, he took a chance and stuck his head in the door.

He saw three live Barubans, a dead one, and a white man.

"Everybody out," he ordered.

"Who are you?" asked Winters.

"All in due time, Mr. Winters. Do any of these gentlemen speak English, do you know?"

Sammy raised his head high and said "I speak much English. Best in my country except for Willem."

"Who the devil is Willem?" asked Mullin.

Sammy pointed to the dead man. "He is Willem."

"He *was* Willem, you mean," Mullin said with a laugh. He waved his .45 at the four survivors and said, "All right, now, all out."

He backed up and allowed the four men to jump out, one at a time. When Winters saw Sands's body, he closed his eyes and shook his head.

Poor Bart. And his poor wife and child.

And poor me, he thought. He looked up at Mullin and said: "Listen, pally, what's the story on this thing, if you don't mind my asking?"

"Not at all," said Mullin. "We are instigating a coup."

"On Baruba?" asked Winters. "A coup?"

Mullin began laughing. He held the .45 loosely in his hand, but the four blacks had Winters and the Barubans covered with their weapons.

"Wouldn't that be something?" Mullin asked, still laughing. "Seizing power on Baruba? What the hell would we do with the bloody thing? Turn it into an outhouse?"

"Well, then, why are we so important?" Winters asked.

Mullin stopped laughing and his face sobered. He squinted at Winters, as if examining him, then said, "Actually, now that you mention it, you're not really that important."

Damn. Winters cursed inwardly. He knew what was coming now, and he launched himself at Mullin hoping the Barubans would follow his lead. Mullin laughed again and fired a .45 slug into the top of Winters's skull. Winters collapsed in a heap with his legs tangled across those of the dead Bart Sands. The Barubans hadn't moved.

"I challenge you," Sammy said suddenly, taking one step toward Mullin. The lieutenant held up his hand to his men so they would not kill the Baruban.

"What's your name, lad?" Mullin asked.

"Sammy Wanenko."

"You're the big mucky-muck athlete?"

"I am Baruba's champion."

"And you want to challenge me?"

"Yes."

"To what?"

"To fight."

Mullin laughed.

"All right, Baruba's greatest athlete, we'll fight." He turned toward his men and said, "I can use the exercise. None of you boys have acted up in a while and I might be getting rusty."

He removed his hat, then motioned to Sammy to step forward. As Sammy neared, Mullin removed his eyeglasses and reached down to put them on his hat. But Wanenko stayed just beyond the range of Mullin's foot, and Mullin stood up again.

"You free us if I win?" Sammy said.

Mullin shrugged. "But of course, lad. To the victor belongs the spoils."

"I do not know what that means, but I fight."

Sammy put his hands in front of him in a boxing stance and he knew that today he must use his right hand. He could not save it for the Olympic games because it was just as important to him today. Mullin turned his palms toward his face and raised his hands in a karate stance, and when Sammy faked a left jab, then threw an overhand right, Mullin backstepped and delivered a front kick that caught Sammy in the stomach. The blow should have felled him on the spot, but Wanenko's youthful strength pumped adrenalin into his body, and after recoiling slightly from the kick, he charged forward, wrapped his arms around Mullin, and let his weight carry the small Briton to the sand.

He drew his right arm back to smash in Mullin's face, just as Mullin reached alongside his body and drew the .45 from its holster. Just as Sammy let the punch fly, Mullin put a bullet up under his throat that smashed up into his brain. Sammy's last thought was that he would not win a gold medal for Baruba.

Mullin pushed the dead body off him and shook his head, angered with himself. The four Africans with him would tell the story of how the young Baruban had challenged him and would have won, had it not been for the gun. And then there would be more and more challenges to Mullin's authority. It wouldn't do, and on the spot, Mullin decided that the four Africans would never again return to the camp of Jimbobwu Mkombu. They would be left behind in Moscow somehow.

He looked at the two remaining Barubans and

said, "You boys didn't want to go to the Olympics anyway." Then he stepped back, out of the line of fire, and motioned to his men. Tonny and Tomas were drilled through the head by bullets, even before they knew what was happening. There were no last-minute thoughts of Olympic gold for them. Their minds had gone numb with fear long before.

They simply died.

"All right, lads, let's get them undressed before they bleed on your clothes." After his men had changed clothes with the Barubans, he made them hide the bodies in the deep brush that ringed the tropical beach.

Then he watched as his men very carefully loaded bags of equipment onto the DC-3. They handled the bags of explosives, molded into the shape of athletic equipment, as if they were newborn babes, which was just the way he wanted them handled.

Those newborn babes will be our love notes to the Americans, he thought. Love notes from Jim Bob Mkombu, delivered by yours truly, Flight Lieutenant Jack Mullin.

A delivery boy? Is that what I really am? he asked himself, but then put the thought behind him. His day would come, he knew. And not far off either.

The coded message came to Jimbobwu Mkombu soon after he had finished dividing his dinner, half into his mouth and the other half onto his shirtfront.

He laughed aloud when he read it. The message was from Mullin and it read: "The Battle of Waterloo was won on the playing fields of Eton."

A success. The first phase of the mission had been a success. His assassins were on their way to Moscow.

Mkombu went to the window and looked over the clearing where a few of his soldiers lounged desultorily.

As he knew they would, the press of the world had jumped upon the story of the threat to the American athletes and had accepted totally the fiction that the threats had been made by some unhappy group of whites in South Africa and Rhodesia. That was the first stick in place. The second was the smuggling of his assassins into Moscow, disguised as Baruban athletes. The third and final stick would be the killing of the Americans.

Nothing the South Africans or the Rhodesians could do would stop the downfall of their regimes after that. And then Jimbobwu Mkombu would be king.

And Mullin?

Mkombu told himself that Flight Lieutenant Jack Mullin's usefulness would some come to an end. He knew that Mullin believed he was just using Mkombu to further his own ends.

In the empty room, Mkombu spoke aloud to himself.

"Soon, he will find who is user and who is used."

CHAPTER EIGHT

The Folcroft estate in Rye, New York, had been built behind thick walls by a millionaire who had no wish to share with the public his passion for young women. It had been used by the United States government during World War II as a training camp for spies, and then had drifted into some kind of vague medical administration headquarters for the government, until one Friday, when all the personnel were told to clear out by 6 P.M. Sunday. Everything would be shipped to their homes, along with their new work assignments.

At 6:01 P.M. that Sunday, Dr. Harold W. Smith, presented by the president of the United States with an assignment he didn't want, arrived at the rickety old dock behind the main Folcroft building. CURE was born.

Over the years, the estate was converted by Smith into Folcroft Sanitarium, an expensive rest home for wealthy malingerers, and it pleased Smith inordinately that he made the sanitarium show an annual profit. This was not really necessary because the sanitarium served only as a front for the massive computer network that was used by CURE in the battle against crime.

Smith's office was in a rear room on the main building's second floor, overlooking the waters of Long Island Sound, which looked bleak, cold, and gray twelve months of the year.

Smith was in his office, patiently explaining what CURE had done about the note threatening America's athletes. Remo sat on a hard-backed chair facing Smith, but Chiun walked back and forth across the room, stopping only to drum his fingers impatiently on Smith's desk.

"I've checked everything," Smith said, "and we just can't tie the terrorist threat to either South Africa or Rhodesia."

"Or anybody else for that matter," Remo suggested. When Smith nodded, Remo said, "For this, the taxpayers spend how many millions a year?"

"Not on me," Chiun said quickly, looking up from drumming on the desk. "Everyone knows how little the Master of Sinanju is recompensed for his efforts in this very wealthy country. It is one of the disgraces of my life. Can we go to Russia now?"

"Just a moment, Master," Smith said. He wondered why Chiun was so anxious to leave. All his enthusiasm for this Moscow mission was making the CURE director suspicious.

"The early bird catches the worm," Chiun said. He nodded toward Remo. "Or, in this case, the early worm may catch the gold medal. We will return in glorious triumph."

Smith cleared his throat. "Yes, well, Remo, what I'm saying is that we don't know who's involved."

"As usual. Come on, Chiun, we're going."

He stood up and Smith said quickly, "I think it would be best if you kept a low profile in Moscow."

"That will be difficult with that big white nose," Chiun said.

"He's telling me not to win anything, Little Father," Remo explained.

Chiun looked at Smith with an expression that meant he thought Smith should be instantly admitted to an asylum.

"What?" he exclaimed. "Lose?"

Smith shrugged. "How would it look if Remo won on national television?"

"Glorious," said Chiun. "Unless he was sloppy, but I will train him to make sure that does not happen."

"Maybe glorious but definitely dangerous," said Smith. "Our secrecy would be in danger. Remo's life in jeopardy. You can understand that, can't you?"

"Of course, I can understand it," Chiun said. "I am not a child."

"Good," Smith said. He told Remo, "Remember, we haven't discounted anybody. Not the South Africans or the Rhodesians or anybody else. We'll keep looking. And Chiun?"

"Yes."

"Thank you for understanding."

"You do not thank someone for being intelligent, Emperor," Chiun said. "It is because I am so intelligent that I understand these things and can sympathize with your plight."

As the two men left his office, Smith began to worry again. Chiun had given up too easily and Smith vowed to be sure to watch the Olympics on television, an instrument he generally disdained.

Out in the hallway, Chiun said to Remo, "That man becomes more and more of a lunatic every day. Imagine. Losing."

In the car driving to Kennedy Airport, Remo asked, "What are you smirking about, Chiun?"

"The Master of Sinanju does not smirk. He smiles in warm appreciation of his own genius."

"And what has your genius come up with now?"

"I have a plan that will make me a star without that lunatic Smith being able to blame us."

"I'll let make-you-a-star pass and just ask what it is you expect me to do," Remo said.

Chiun rubbed his dry, long-nailed hands together in unrestrained enjoyment. "We will physically disable all the other American athletes. Not seriously. I know how squeamish you are about these things. Just enough so that they can't compete. Then you will enter all the events and win all the gold medals and you will tell the world you owe it all to me, your trainer, and then I will do endorsements on television and get rich."

"Brilliant," Remo said.

"Of course," said Chiun.

"Except for one thing."

"Name that thing," Chiun demanded.

"I won't do it."

"I beg your pardon." Chiun's voice was outrage itself.

"Smitty'd never buy all our athletes getting sick or hurt in an accident. Not all of them."

Chiun frowned. "Hmmmm," he said. "Maybe half of them."

"None of them," Remo said. "It'd be too suspicious. Smith'd see through it right away and if he even suspected that you had anything to do with anything that messed up our Olympic team, it could mean the end of that lovely submarine of gold that arrives in Sinanju every November."

"There are rare occasions, white thing, when you almost make sense. We will think of something else."

Chiun sank back into the passenger's seat in silence. His next idea was not long in coming and it was even better, but he decided not to tell it to Remo, who had that hangdog loser mentality of Americans, always finding reasons why things couldn't be done.

His new idea would be to disable not just the American athletes but all the athletes of the world. Remo would be the winner by default.

Chiun liked this plan even better.

CHAPTER NINE

This was the new Russia. Receding into the mists of history were the bloody millions-dead purges of a Stalin and the random cruelties of a Khrushchev. The bloodshed aimed at its own people had largely stopped. But the successors of Stalin and Khrushchev were still paranoidal xenophobes and a call to the Kremlin was still an occasion for sweaty palms on the part of most Russians.

For one thing never changed, new Russia or old Russia. Some of the people called to the Kremlin never came back.

But when the call came for Dimitri Sorkofsky, a colonel in the KGB, Russia's secret police, he merely wondered why it had taken them so long to call.

Sorkofsky was a prideful man, proud of his service record, as he was proud of his two small daughters, Nina, eleven, and Marta, seven. He had been equally proud of their mother, his beautiful Natasha, until she had died five years earlier at the age of thirty-two.

As he walked through the Moscow streets toward his appointment, Sorkofsky knew he was going to be given the greatest assignment of his career, and his sole regret was that Natasha was not there to share it with him.

Natasha had been fifteen years younger than he and she had always been so filled with life that she had kept him young. He never knew what had made her fall in love with an ugly old bear of a man like him, but he was only happy that she had. Happy and proud. He recalled how his chest puffed with pride anytime he went anywhere with Natasha on his arm, anytime he saw other men's eyes follow her across a room. And then she was told she had incurable bone cancer.

Still, during those last six months, she had been the strong one and after she had died, he felt guilty that somehow she had made those six months the happiest of his life when, by all rights, they should have been the saddest. But she would not hear of sad. She had nothing to be sad about, she had told Dimitri. She had raised two lovely daughters and had a lovely, lovely man for a husband.

He paused on the street and rubbed a hand over the lumps that seemed to have piled up to form his face. How could she have felt that way about him? He touched his eyes with his hand, found moisture, and wiped it away.

Dimitri Sorkofsky was called "The Rhino." He was six-foot-three and weighed 250 pounds. His Neanderthal brow belied his high intelligence. His hands were like massive paws, and yet Natasha had often called them the gentlest hands in the world. Her love for him had found beauty where there was none for others to see.

He had been so proud of her, just as he was proud of his skills, and when he reported to his superiors in the Kremlin and was told that he would be in charge of security for the Olympic Games, he was, oddly, not thrilled—first, because he thought he was simply the most qualified man for the job, and second, because Natasha was not there to share in his glory.

His superior, a man with eyebrows like black hedges, told him that a decision had been made at the highest levels on the Americans' request to send their own security people to protect their threatened athletes.

"And that decision is?" asked Sorkofsky.

"That decision is no. The American imperialists would only seize that opportunity to flood our country with their CIA spies."

Sorkofsky nodded, silently wondering to himself if his superior really believed that claptrap, and knowing it didn't really matter. The Americans would send agents anyway. He knew it because it was what he would have done under the same circumstances.

He was wished well in his new assignment. He had just begun to assemble a staff when he was informed again by his superior that the Americans had protested to the premier and a compromise had been reached. Another man would be added to his security force, a West German police captain named Wilhelm Bechenbauer.

"That's all right," Sorkofsky said. "I can work with him."

"You know this man?" his superior asked, suddenly suspicious.

"No. But I can work with anybody."

Captain Wilhelm Bechenbauer did not like being assigned to Russia. He did not like being away from his family that long.

His son was of high school age and his wife, a good woman quite capable of raising their twelve-year-old daughter, Helga, was not equipped to handle fifteen-year-old Hans. That boy needed the strong hand of a father.

Bechenbauer was a dapper, well-dressed, trim man of five-foot-seven whose weight never varied more than a pound from 140. He sported an impeccably trimmed mustache and he too had a nickname. He was called "The Ferret."

The Ferret was looking forward to meeting the

Rhino, and the longer he thought about it, the more he looked forward to something else about his Moscow assignment: Russian women. He had never had a Russian woman and he was looking forward to it. At forty-six, Bechenbauer was as lusty as he had been at twenty-six, and while this pleased him, it seemed to irritate his wife. He managed, nevertheless, to make do.

Captain Bechenbauer had been in Colonel Sorkofsky's outer office for twenty minutes and he knew that it was no accident that he was being forced to wait so long. Sorkofsky was establishing their relative positions early in their relationship. Bechenbauer thought to himself that it was a needless display. He was perfectly willing to let the Russian run the show. He lit one of his favorite cigars and sat back with his legs crossed, pleased to find that the colonel's secretary was attractive. Perhaps she would be the one to introduce him to the world of Russian women.

Sorkofsky thought that half an hour was long enough to keep the West German waiting. He was about to buzz his secretary but decided to go outside and welcome Bechenbauer himself. The West German, if he was as smart as his dossier seemed to indicate, would know what Sorkofsky had done.

When he opened the door, he saw a smallish man sitting on the edge of his secretary's desk. Both were laughing. He noticed the wedding band on Bechenbauer's left hand and took an immediate dislike to the German. Away from home only one day and already looking to play love games. The colonel had never cheated on his wife, neither in life nor in death, and he detested any man who would.

"Captain Bechenbauer, I presume," he said loudly. His secretary jumped and looked sheepish. Bechenbauer looked at Sorkofsky, at the girl, and then back to the KGB colonel. He was frowning when he slid off her desk and approached the larger man with his hand outstretched.

"I am pleased to meet you, Colonel. I have heard many good things about you."

Sorkofsky turned away from the German's hand.

"Come inside, Captain," he said and walked to his desk. Behind him, he heard Bechenbauer whisper something to his secretary and became even more annoyed.

When Bechenbauer was in the office, Sorkofsky curtly commanded: "Sit." The West German obeyed and looked at the Russian colonel with an amused look on his face.

"We have a problem already, Colonel, and we have just met?" he asked in flawless Russian.

"It is your problem if you toss yourself onto other women the moment you are away from your wife," Sorkofsky said.

"I am sorry if I poached on your private preserve," Bechenbauer said.

For a moment, Sorkofsky did not understand the idiom, then his face reddened and he leaped to his feet.

"Miss Kamirov is my secretary and nothing more, Captain, and I object to your implication."

"Then I apologize for the implication," Bechenbauer said. "However, I do not apologize for my behavior, which is none of your business. We are here to work on a mission. I will not attempt to change your life habits and I would appreciate it if you would not attempt to change mine. I will tell you only that I love my wife in my own way. I will not discuss it further."

Sorkofsky blinked rapidly while looking at the smaller man across his desk. The German confused him. He seemed sincere about his love of his wife and yet he cheated on her. Sorkofsky threw his hands up in the air with a smile.

"Captain, I apologize too. I did not mean to lose my temper. It does not often occur. It will not again."

Bechenbauer transferred his cigar from his right hand to his left hand, stood up and stepped up to the colonel. He extended his right hand.

"In that case, perhaps we can start again with a handshake."

Sorkofsky met the Germans' eyes again and together they smiled before shaking hands like old friends.

"Good," said Sorkofsky.

"And I want you to know that I understand you are in charge of this operation. I am here only to help you in any way I can."

"Thank you." The two men returned to their seats. "You know why you are here?"

"I know that the Americans asked permission to send their agents to protect their athletes. I know that your country refused. I know that the Americans had me designated to come in as an advisor. I also know that this is supposed to lull all you Russians to sleep so that you will never guess that American agents will be sent in anyway."

Sorkofsky grinned.

"You are very perceptive," he said.

Bechenbauer smiled back. "No problem," he said. "If the Americans run their spy system the way they run their foreign policy, we need only look for the athletes wearing trenchcoats and carrying daggers. They will be easy to find. I think our biggest problem will be keeping them out from underfoot."

"My opinion exactly," the big Russian said. "You were at Munich?"

Bechenbauer's face lost the faint smile that habitually played at the corners of his mouth. "Yes, Colonel. I wish I could tell you what the horrors of Munich were like."

97

"I have been in war, Captain. I know what bodies look like."

"I'm sure you do," the German said, "but we are not talking of dead soldiers, killed in battle. We are talking about young people who came to Munich to compete in games and were greeted with death. To such as you and I, violence is a way of life. But these were children. That is why I am here. I volunteered because I feel I have something to atone for."

"Why you? You were not on the security team at Munich," the Russian said.

"It was my country in which this atrocity occurred," Bechenbauer said. Sorkofsky was confused by the man but could not doubt his sincerity. How strange that the man could be so sensitive in one way and in another, he had no sensitivity at all. Unless alley cats were to be considered sensitive.

"I understand," he said. "Perhaps you will rest at your hotel and in the morning, we can review our plans."

"That is kind of you, Colonel." With a smile, Bechenbauer added, "Perhaps I may even find some young lady who will show me your Russian nightlife."

The man was incorrigible, Sorkofsky decided, but before he could say anything, the small German had left his office.

Bechenbauer was curious too about Colonel Sorkofsky and he asked Miss Kamirov about him after they had made love for the second time that night.

"Your colonel intrigues me, Ilya."

"Oh?" she asked, blinking her large brown eyes at him. They were in bed in his hotel room, where they had ended up after cruising several of Moscow's dull nightclubs. Ilya was taller than Bechenbauer and more than twenty years younger, but she made no attempt to hide her attraction to him. Most women were attracted to him, and she had been surprised at the ferocity with which he made love. He was better and more adept than any young man she had ever encountered and she had encountered her share, for she enjoyed sex.

"Why does he intrigue you?" she asked.

"He seems such a rigid moralist. Is he always like that?"

"So far as I know. I am told he was devoted to his late wife. Now his life is his two daughters."

"He has never made a pass at you?" Bechenbauer asked.

"Never. I tried to get him to but he never seemed to notice. Finally I gave up."

Bechenbauer nodded. So Sorkofsky was for real. For some reason, he felt pleased. He might never like the Russian but he could respect him as an honest man.

Rolling over atop Ilya, he began to think the time he spent in Russia might not be so hard to take after all.

Sorkofsky had tucked his girls in after telling them a bedtime story, and then gone to his den, where he smoked his only pipe of the day and drank his only vodka. He kept it in the small freezer section of his den's refrigerator, which helped to thicken the liquid into a velvety soft relaxant.

He thought of Bechenbauer as he sipped. He had originally been wary of the man, suspecting that he might be an undercover American spy in Russia to coordinate the efforts of all the American spies. But he had rejected that idea now. His life with Communist conspiracy theory had taught him one thing: generally the simplest explanation is the accurate one. Bechenbauer was a German security officer, no more, no less. And from his file, a very good one.

The doorbell interrupted his muse. A military

messenger was on his doorstep. He seemed surprised to see the Rhinoceros in pajamas and bathrobe.

"Sorry to disturb you, Colonel, but Lieutenant Protchik thought you should see this tonight."

Protchik was one of Sorkofsky's aides, an ambitious young soldier who did everything he could to keep on the colonel's good side. Sorkofsky detested him.

He took the envelope and thanked the corporal. He waited until he was back in his study before he opened the envelope and read the contents.

It was another note from the S.A.A.E. The note had just been received by the president of the United States, Protchik advised him in a cover memo.

The note to the president read:

"Everything is in place. As a lesson to the imperialist cowards of America who flee their friends at the first sign of trouble, let it be known that not one American athlete will return from Moscow alive. All will die."

The note was postmarked Salisbury, Rhodesia. The first note, Sorkofsky knew, had been sent from Pretoria, South Africa.

Sorkofsky read the note several times, then telephoned Bechenbauer's hotel.

A woman answered the insistent ringing in the German officer's room.

"Let me speak to Captain Bechenbauer," Sorkofsky ordered stiffly.

The woman seemed confused and stuttered a moment, then Bechenbauer came onto the line.

"Yes, Colonel."

"Something has come up. Can you be in my office at 6 A.M.?"

"Of course, Colonel."

Sorkofsky hesitated. He thought he should say something to the German about his deplorable morals.

100

"Will that be all, Colonel?" Bechenbauer asked.

Angrily, Sorkofsky snapped, "Yes. Until tomorrow. But for God's sake, man, try to get some sleep."

He slammed down the telephone and walked upstairs to his bedroom. Something was bothering him. He shouldn't have acted so brusquely with Bechenbauer. What was it?

The woman. Her voice had sounded familiar and had seemed flustered when she heard Sorkofsky. Did she recognize his voice? She must have. How had Bechenbauer known it was him on the telephone when he had not identified himself?

Was it—? No. Not his secretary. He told himself he must stop conjuring up ghosts. He had enough real problems to deal with.

CHAPTER TEN

Remo had seen it in the Caribbean, and he expected it in South America and Africa, but he hadn't expected it when he and Chiun stepped off the Russian Aeroflot liner at Moscow's Airport. Beggars.

"Choon gum, mister?" asked a young boy with a blond head so square that it looked as if he had been raised in a Kleenex box. When Remo shook his head, the boy did not even acknowledge it, but instead just moved farther down along the line of American athletes who had arrived on the plane, asking in his few words of English, "Choon gum, candy?"

Remo and Chiun followed the line into the main airport terminal. A young man about Remo's size with thin sandy hair and the face of a mob scene extra sidled up to him.

"You got jeans?" he asked. "Hundred dollars American if you got jeans."

"I don't wear jeans," Remo said.

"Whatchoocall whatchoowear? Chinos? Fifty dollars American for chinos?" the young Russian said.

"No," said Remo. "I'm wearing them myself."

"How about a robe?" Chiun said to the man. "Like mine." Almost reverently, he touched the blue brocaded robe he wore. "Maybe a little thinner. Just what you need for your summers. Fifty dollars. I brought extras."

"No wear robe," the man said. "Need jeans, chinos. Got buyer for jeans, chinos. You got jeans, chinos, mister?"

"Be gone, primitive," Chiun said. He turned his back on the man and spoke to Remo.

"These people have nothing to wear?" he asked.

"Sure. If they all want to wear khaki pants," Remo said. "American clothes are what they want."

"What kind of country is this?" Chiun said.

"Just a vision of a glorious new tomorrow of brotherhood and freedom," said Remo, reading from a brochure that Russian travel guides were shoving into the hands of all the athletes.

"This is stupid. It was never like this under Ivan the Wonderful," Chiun said.

"Welcome to Russia," said Remo. "You have seen the future and the only thing that works in it is you and me."

The Russians had decided that security checks would be made at the Olympic village, not at the airport, and the athletic contingent was herded through the terminal toward waiting buses. As they moved in lime, Remo noticed a long queue of people standing alongside one of the far walls.

Chiun saw them too.

"What is that?" he said. He walked away from the athletes toward the far line.

Remo followed him. "It's a line. Come on, Chiun, we've got to go."

"Not yet," Chiun said. "If there is a line, it means there is something good at the end of it. I know about lines, Remo. I have seen this before. We will stand in this line."

"Come on, Chiun. Whatever they're selling, you won't want. Let's hit it."

"Nonsense," Chiun said. "You never really learn anything, do you, Remo? I tell you, there is something good at the end of this line."

Remo sighed. "You wait in line. I'll go up front and see what they're selling."

"Yes," Chiun said. "Do that and report back to me." As Remo walked away, he called out: "And check the price."

"Yes sir," Remo said.

At the end of the line, there was a counter that looked like an American newsstand with a hand-painted sign in Russian over it. Remo could not read the sign but he could see what the people were buying: cigarettes. English cigarettes, Players, in a cardboard box. One pack each.

"Cigarettes," he told Chiun.

"I don't believe it," Chiun said. He folded his arms. "Why would anyone wait in line for cigarettes?"

"Because it's hard to get foreign cigarettes in Russia and Russian cigarettes taste as if they're made from cow flop. Take my word for it, Chiun, they're selling cigarettes."

"That is terrible. What a tragedy."

"Yes."

"If we had known cigarettes would have been such a hit, we could have brought some with us and sold them," said Chiun.

"Next time maybe," Remo said.

They walked back toward the line of American athletes slogging slowly toward the waiting buses. As he glanced around, Remo noticed that almost all of the Americans were being accosted by young Russians. He could hear some of the words. They were being offered hard cash for their blue jeans, cash for their Mickey Mouse sweatshirts, money for loose cigarettes they might have, money for gum or candy or digital LED watches.

"Next time we come, remember to bring cigarettes," Chiun said definitively. "And a lot of the other junk these people seem to want."

"I will," Remo said. He had read stories about Russia's sacrificing consumer interests to spend money on defense, but they had been just words to him until he had seen for himself how that policy translated into reality for the Russian man on the street.

That impression was reinforced as they rode through Moscow on buses. Everywhere, Remo saw lines, stretching out the front door of stores and half-way down the block. And he saw people carrying out their precious packages after having successfully out-lasted the line. A few packs of cigarettes. Pantyhose. One woman carried a brassiere in her hand and her face was set in a look of tigerish triumph.

Remo and Chiun were assigned a room together in a large cinderblock building that was inside the miles of fencing that surrounded the Olympic village built just outside Moscow.

As they stepped inside the room, both felt the vibrations immediately. Remo looked toward Chiun but Chiun was already walking toward the far wall where there was a lamp alongside one of the small bunks. With the side of his hand, Chiun slapped at the base of the lamp and ripped it from the wall. He reached in among the tangled wires and brought forth a little silver disc.

"So much for the hidden microphone," Remo said. "But . . ."

"You are correct. There is more," Chiun said. Over a large dresser against the side wall was a four-foot-high mirror. Remo felt, sensed without under-standing why, some vibration from the mirror. As he went toward it, Chiun was ahead of him. The Orien-tal felt along the right side of the mirror. Remo thought it odd that the mirror was anchored directly to the wall and not to the dresser.

Chiun ran his long thin fingers along the right edge of the mirror. When he reached the top of the wood frame, he nodded to himself and with a sudden splash outward of his fingertips, broke off the top right corner of the mirror. He looked at it and tossed it toward Remo, who caught it, turned it over, and saw that that section of the mirror had been made of one-way glass. He looked at the bare wall exposed by the broken glass. A small camera lens was built into the wall. Chiun reached his fingertips toward the wall. He caught the metal frame housing the lens between two fingers and squeezed. The metal slowly bent shut. Inside the little tube of metal, Remo could hear the glass lens being cracked and shattered to powder.

"There," said Chiun. "Now we are alone."

"Good," said Remo. "You come here often?"

"What?"

"Forget it," Remo said. "It's a thing people say in the States. At singles bars." When he saw Chiun's blank look, he shrugged and shook his head. Forget it. You had to be there."

"Something is on your mind," Chiun said, "that you are so intent on playing games these days."

Remo dropped onto the single bed near the window. He knew he had his choice of the two beds because Chiun slept on the floor on an old grass mat. He had to admit it to himself that Chiun was right on the mark. Something was on Remo's mind. Josie Littlefeather. He tried to put her out of his head.

"Now that we're here," he said, "we've got to keep our eyes open for terrorists." He looked out the window at the gray Russian sky. It reminded him of Smith's personality. "I wonder how they're going to try to get into the games."

"The story is told by the Greatest Master Wang," Chiun said.

Remo groaned. "Please, Chiun. No fables."

"How quick you are to label history a fable," Chiun said. "Didn't you just ask a question?"

108

"Yes. I wondered how the terrorists were going to get into the games. I didn't ask what the Great Wang had for dinner two thousand years ago."

"It was longer than that," Chiun said. "And you know what they say, don't you?"

"What do they say?"

"They say that those who do not remember history are condemned to have to listen to it more than once. The Greatest Master Wang was a great athlete, as are all Masters of Sinanju. But of course, the Greatest Master Wang, being the Greatest Master, was also the greatest athlete in the history of Sinanju."

Their room was three stories up. Remo knew he could open the window, jump to the ground, and live. But that would not change his fate. It would delay the inevitable. Remo figured he could change his name and run away. He could hide among the Bedouins of northern Africa for ten years. And when he decided to return to the States, one winter night, at 2 A.M., when he walked into a hotel room in some dismal southern state, Chiun would be there, sitting on the floor, and he would say: "As I was saying, the Greatest Master Wang was the greatest athlete of all the Masters of Sinanju." And he would go on without missing a beat as if nothing had happened.

Remo decided to get it over with now. He pretended to listen.

"This was before the time of these Western games, these Olympics as you call them.

"In those days, there was a sporting competition held in Korea among the many cities. And it happened that two of these cities were constantly at war with each other, even though they called a truce during the games because the games themselves were a time of great good will among men.

"So, one night, while the Greatest Master Wang was home, eating a soup of fish and rice of which he was most fond—he cooked this soup with a very spicy red pepper which grew then in that part of the country. A nice soup, with a special warming character. Still, not intrusive. It was—"

"Chiun, please," Remo said. "Skip the soup and do the story."

"You care nothing about beauty," said Chiun.

"I care nothing about soup."

"At any rate, the people of the first city came to the master and said to him that they wanted him to ingratiate himself with the rulers of the second city so that he could compete on the second city's behalf in these athletic games. Do you understand so far?"

"Yes, City A said to Wang, you go compete on behalf of City B."

"These cities were not named City A and City B," Chiun said. "They were named—"

"Go ahead," said Remo. "I'm listening. Skip the cities as well as the soup."

"So Master Wang did as he was commissioned and he competed on behalf of the second city and of course won all the events. In most of them, the champion he had to defeat came from the first city, the city which had retained him."

"Why? Why would the first city hire Wang?"

"The Greatest Master Wang," Chiun corrected.

"Why would the first city hire the Greatest Master Wang to defeat them? That doesn't make sense."

"Just be quiet and let me finish."

"Go ahead," Remo said.

"When the Greatest Master Wang won every event, he was carried back to the second city as a hero. The people of the second city asked him what he wished as tribute to his great skill, which had brought them such honor. He told them he wanted their respect. He suggested that they cut a hole in the wall of their city as a symbol, because with such a great master as Wang as their champion, who needed city walls for safety?

"So the leaders of that city broke a hole in the wall of their fortifications. When they showed him the wall, the Greatest Master scoffed. Such a small hole for such a great hero was an insult. The hole was made larger, much larger. That night when all slept, the Greatest Master Wang left the second city and went home. Later in the night, soldiers from the first city marched through the hole in the wall and disposed of all their enemies in the second city."

"Old Wang's a sweetheart," Remo said. "And the moral of this story is, don't ever trust a Master of Sinanju."

"There are many morals to this story and that is not one of them. First of all, the Greatest Master Wang did what he was retained to do. To break through the defenses of the second city. He did that. And he did it with style. In fact, I think that the Greeks adopted the custom for their Olympic games. Without paying. Nobody ever pays Sinanju for any of the things they steal from us."

"All right, all right. What has this got to do with terrorists?"

"Sometimes I think you are truly denser than stone. The Greatest Master Wang knew that the best way to break into someplace was to be inside in the first place."

"I don't understand what that has to do with anything."

"Stone," Chiun muttered. "Denser than stone."

CHAPTER ELEVEN

The list of "Official Rules For Visiting Olympic Athletes" was slid under Remo and Chiun's door ten minutes after they arrived in their room.

The list, printed in a tiny type face called Brilliant, which had not been used for a century in the United States for anything except shipping news and the lifetime records of also-ran horses, took up both sides of six sheets of pink paper.

"What does it say?" asked Chiun.

"I don't know. I don't have a year to read it," Remo said. "Try this, though. Don't try to leave the Olympic village. Don't talk to anybody. Don't take pictures. Rat on anybody who does those things. And don't even consider trying to beat the glorious athletes from the glorious Communist countries. If you want to defect, call for an appointment. They promise to get you on television. And there will be a bus ride in twenty minutes and all will go."

"I'm not going," Chiun said. "Russia is very depressing. Any country that stands in line for cigarettes has nothing to show me that I want to see."

"I'll probably go," Remo said. He was thinking of Josie Littlefeather. She should be on the bus ride.

Chiun looked at him suspiciously. "Yes, you go," he said. "Tell me of anything interesting."

"Will you be all right here alone?" Remo felt, unaccountably, suddenly guilty.

"Of course I'll be all right. I don't mind being

114

alone. In truth I have been alone since first I had the misfortune to encounter you. I will stay here and rest. Then I will walk around the village. Not for me the idle pursuits of youth. I will be about, doing my emperor's business. I will . . ."

"See you later, Chiun," Remo said as he walked toward the door. There was a kind of overkill of guilt common to both Jewish mothers and Korean assassins that, after a while, roused not guilt but amusement. Remo no longer felt guilty.

He waited at the staging area, where a long line of red, lumpy-looking buses without air conditioning were lined up. Secret policemen trying unsuccessfully to imitate tour guides kept trying to herd Remo onto one of the buses but he kept ignoring them, watching and waiting for Josie Littlefeather.

She walked up about twenty minutes later, part of a group of female gymnasts from the United States, and Remo was again struck by how much bigger and more mature she was than the rest of them.

Her face brightened when she saw him and Remo waved casually at her, trying to make it seem as if he had not been waiting for her but had just happened onto the scene.

She smiled and said, "Been waiting long?"

"Just got here," he said. She stared at him with a slight smile still toying with the corners of her mouth. "Twenty minutes," he confessed.

"Good," she said. "It gives me a sense of power. You haven't forgotten that you owe me some instruction on the balance beam."

"Put it out of your head. You're a guaranteed winner," Remo said. "You taking the tour?"

"They didn't seem to leave much choice on that executive order." She mimicked a Russian accent. "You vill show up at 2 P.M. for the bus tour of beautiful downtown Moscow. You vill not take pictures. You vill blow no bridges around here, American."

115

Remo laughed then. "Let's go then. Mustn't disappoint our Russian hosts."

They sat in a back seat of a bus together, trying without much success to ignore their Russian guide who extolled the virtues of living in a Communist state over a handheld loudspeaker whose output would have shamed a New York disco.

"I don't mind comic book Karl Marx," Remo told Josie, "but top volume is a drag."

"He's talking loud so you won't notice the lines outside all the stores and how badly the people are dressed."

Remo glanced out the window and saw that Josie was right. The Russian cityscape looked like an old newsreel of Depression America. The people wore lumpy, shapeless clothing.

"It looks like a black and white movie," Remo said. "Grim."

"There is grimness in America too," Josie said. "My people have that look too. Maybe people who are held down, told to stay in their so-called place, have that look the world over."

"Don't start on that," Remo said. "I don't believe it first of all. And even if it was true, it's not my fault. I wasn't at Wounded Ankle or whatever the hell it is you people are always complaining about."

Josie started to answer when the guide told them in his loud, baritone, unaccented English that they were at the Tretyakov Gallery, one of the world's great museums, and that they would disembus now and go look at paintings for twenty minutes.

As they got up to leave the bus, Remo said, "Now we'll split."

"We'll get in trouble," she warned.

"Naaah," Remo said. "We'll be back at the Village before they are. We'll just tell them we got lost if anybody asks."

"If you say so," she said.

116

The crowd of athletes turned left off the bus to follow the guide and Remo and Josie turned right and crossed the street toward a group of shops. Immediately Remo knew they were being followed. He decided not to mention it to Josie.

"Maybe we shouldn't have," she said.

"Don't worry about it."

"We won't get arrested or anything?"

"Not for strolling around," Remo said. By their reflection in a store window, he saw two men following them. They wore brightly flowered shirts and pants that bagged at the knees.

He darted with Josie into the doorway of a store. They stood behind a counter, looking over medallions of Lenin and heroic tractor drivers, and only a few seconds later, the two men entered the store.

Remo pulled Josie down toward the floor. He heard the men walk by on the other side of the counter. Quickly, he stood up, pulled Josie to the door, and they went out into the street.

"What's that all about?" she asked.

"Just shaking our tail," he said.

They went into another shop three doors farther down. It sold medallions of Karl Marx and of heroic tractor drivers. They waited there for two minutes until the two men in flowered shirts passed them. Remo was surprised that in the entire two minutes, no salesperson came up to them to pester them under the pretext of offering help. Perhaps Communism did have something to recommend it after all.

They went back out into the street, walked to the corner and turned left on Bolshaya Ordynka Street. Half a block down they found what looked like the Russian equivalent of a coffee shop and went inside.

A waitress, whose long black dress made her look like the official greeter for a funeral home, finally understood that they wanted coffee, but even as she poured it from an old pottery urn, she kept turning her head to stare at the two obvious foreigners.

"We're being watched," Josie told Remo.

"They're not watching me," he said. "It's you they can't keep their eyes off."

She took his hands in hers and told him, "You're sweet," and Remo wondered how sweet she'd think he was if she knew about the past ten years, all the deaths, all the bodies.

"Why are you running track?" she asked him abruptly. "I've seen you on the balance beam. You could win anything in gymnastics."

"I don't know. There's just something about running, I guess," said Remo.

"They talk about you, you know," she said.

"About me?"

"Yes. They call you strange. You dress strange, you act strange, you—"

"What do you think?" Remo asked.

"I told you. I think you're sweet. *And* strange."

"Then I guess I'm strange. What's keeping that coffee?"

He looked toward the counter, just in time to see two soldiers enter the shop. They looked about until their eyes fell on Remo and Josie.

"Company," he told her. He felt her hands tense up and he said, "Don't worry. Just another nosy Communist waitress doing her job."

The soldiers came to the table. One said, "Excuse, please. You are with Olympics?"

"Yes," said Remo.

"You not belong outside Olympic Village by yourself," the soldier informed them. He was looking at Josie's bustline as he spoke. The other soldier was staring at her beautifully boned face. *To each his own,* thought Remo.

"We got lost," Remo said.

"We will take you back," the guard said.

"Thank you," said Remo. He helped Josie from her chair. He turned to the waitress, smiled, waved, and called, "Take poison, bitch."

They followed the soldiers outside, where they were hustled into the back seat of a waiting Army car. It deposited them into the hands of security guards at the main gate of the Olympic village. The guards insisted upon taking their names. Remo gave his name as Abraham Lincoln. Josie said her name was Sacajawea Schwartz.

The guards dutifully wrote the names down, asking to be sure the spelling was correct. Remo told them the spelling was worth a B-plus. Then both he and Josie were back inside the village.

It was dark and there was music all around, the strains of different countries competing in the night-time air.

"Let's go to the gym," Remo said. "We'll start tonight to get you ready."

She nodded and Remo led her to a small practice gymnasium on the outskirts of the main competition complex. The door was locked but Remo slapped it open and the building was dark but Remo found the light panel and flicked on just one small light, enough to illuminate the balance beam apparatus at the far end of the hall.

He had Josie go through her routine and watched her closely. She had trouble with her front walkovers and her split-lift to a handstand.

"Damn," she said as she hopped off the beam. "I just mess up all the time on those."

"You ever do them right?" asked Remo.

"Not often."

"But once in a while?"

"Yeah. Why?"

"If you can do it once, you can do it every time," Remo said. "It doesn't change. You do."

"What do you mean?" she asked.

119

"Josie, all this competition's in your head. The beam is always the same. It never changes. Your body is always the same. The only variable involved is in your head. Get back up on the beam."

She hopped back up and stood there, looking down at him. She had stripped off the skirt she was wearing over her body suit and Remo again felt a tingle looking at her proud woman's body.

"Look at the beam," he said. "How wide is it?"

"Four inches," she said.

"Wrong. That beam is two feet wide. There is no way you can fall off it. Now, down the center of that two-foot beam there's a four-inch red stripe. Do you see it?"

She looked down, hard. "No. I see a four-inch beam."

"Close your eyes," Remo said.

"Okay." She had her eyes screwed tightly together.

"Now see it in your mind," Remo said. "Do you see it? Two-foot-wide beam, a four-inch red stripe."

She laughed. "Yes. I see it. I see it."

"Keep your eyes closed," Remo said. "Okay. Now you do your routine on that two-foot beam, but you try to stay on the four-inch red stripe."

"All right." She walked to the far end of the beam to begin her routine. She looked at Remo before starting and he shook his head. "Not with your eyes open, dummy. With your eyes closed."

"Remo, I can't."

"Yes, you can. Look. Get down off there for a moment," he said, and as she hopped down, lightly, Remo vaulted up onto the beam.

The Russians' list of rules for athletes had explained that all athletes would be treated equally, but, like Animal Farm, some were more equal than others.

Because he came from a Russian satellite country,

East German runner Hans Schlichter had no trouble in getting a key to the locked practice gymnasium. He had told the Russian staff he wanted to do some calisthenics. But, in fact, he wanted privacy to examine the equipment and see if he could devise a way of making his victory in the 800-meter race a sure thing.

He let himself in with the key and when he saw the light on at the end of the gym, pressed himself into the shadows against the wall.

He recognized the American man instantly. All the East German athletes had been given dossiers and photographs of all their potential opponents. It was that Remo Black, and he was considered odd even by his teammates, but what was he doing on the balance beam?

Schlichter watched in amazement as Remo, with his eyes tightly shut, did a flawless routine on the bar beam, and then hopped down where the Indian-looking American woman hugged him and told him he was marvelous.

"So will you be when we're done," Remo said.

Schlichter saw the young woman hold Remo in her arms, then lift her mouth to be kissed. Remo obliged, and even though Schlichter would have liked to stay to watch, he slipped back out through the door, just as the two athletes slid to the practice mat on the floor.

Schlichter had to think about this Remo Black. If he could do such wonders on the balance beam, which was not even a man's event, what might he do on the track?

Something, he decided, would have to be done about that American.

CHAPTER TWELVE

The next morning, Colonel Dimitri Sorkofsky received a message directly from the Southern Africans for Athletic Equality. The contents of the note caused him to summon Captain Bechenbauer to his office immediately.

In the weeks they had been working together, they had not come to understand each other any better but they had learned substantial mutual respect. Each knew the other was a professional.

Sorkofsky was anxious for Bechenbauer to arrive so they could discuss the new note and how to guard against its threat.

Despite what Sorkofsky thought of Bechenbauer's morals, the West German missed his wife very much. In fact, when the telephone summons came from Sorkofsky, the Ferret was reading a letter from his wife. There was a lovely young blonde woman in the bed with him while he was reading it. She was nuzzling his neck and reading over his shoulder.

"She truly misses you," the woman remarked.

The German smiled. "As I miss her and my children. It will not be much longer."

At that point, there was a knock on the hotel room door. Bechenbauer donned his dressing gown and opened the door to the military messenger who was carrying the summons from Sorkofsky.

"The colonel would like you to come to his office at once, sir. He said it was very urgent."

"Thank you, soldier."

The soldier stood there a second too long, his eyes looking past Bechenbauer at the blonde on the bed, who stretched her arms over her head, causing the sheet to slide down and bare her breasts.

Reluctantly, the soldier looked away, saluted Bechenbauer and turned to the door.

"Soldier?" Bechenbauer said.

"Sir?"

"It would not be wise of you to speak of the young lady's presence. Her husband might object. Do you understand?"

The soldier nodded and grinned. "Perfectly, sir. Have no fear."

When he left, Bechenbauer smiled. He knew that in minutes Colonel Sorkofsky would know that there was a blonde in the German's bed. There was no surer way of getting a Russian to carry a message than to ask him not to. They all feared they would be implicated in a spy plot unless they told everything they knew. And it gave the German pleasure to tease the Rhino. Who knew? Before this assignment was over, he might even have brought the big Russian colonel back down to earth, to life as a man.

He went back to the bed, kissed the blonde and ran a finger down her bare breasts, causing her to shiver.

"You were teasing the boy," he scolded.

She reached inside his dressing gown and said "It will give him character." He pulled away from her and said, "I have all the character I need. And duty calls."

She lay in bed watching him as he dressed rapidly.

When he was ready to leave, he asked, "Will you wait?"

"Of course. Where would I go?"

He kissed her goodbye and said, "I will miss you when I return to Germany, *liebchen*."

She kissed him back and said ominously, "We will worry about that another time."

He thought of her on the limousine ride to Sorkofsky's office. She had been a pleasant diversion for him, but he hoped she would not become difficult when it was time for him to leave. He did very much miss his wife.

Sorkofsky was sitting behind his desk in the small office inside the Olympic village when Bechenbauer arrived.

"Your messenger said it was urgent."

"Look at this," the Russian said, handing the note across the desk.

Bechenbauer sat back and read the brief note. Sorkofsky had memorized it and repeated it in his mind. "In the name of Southern Africans for Athletic Equality, we demand the cancellation of the Olympic games. If they are not cancelled, every American athlete will die. To convince you, there will be a show of power on the same day you receive this note. Long live free Rhodesia and South Africa."

"A show of power," Bechenbauer repeated, handing the note back. "Our security is very tight."

"It may be tight only in our minds," the Russian said.

"Why do you say that?"

Sorkofsky ran his hands over his face, dry-washing it, before answering. He felt drained. His younger daughter had run a fever the night before, and he had sat up all night watching her. She was fine this morning, but he had not slept at all and was beginning to feel it.

"There are just too many people from too many countries," he said. "There is no way we can be sure. People are wandering all over the place." He waved at a pile of reports on his desk, then on impulse

126

snatched the first one. "Here. Two Americans wandering around Moscow. Found in a restaurant by soldiers."

"Spies, no doubt," Bechenbauer said. "We knew enough to expect that. But they are not our terrorists." His curiosity was piqued anyway. "Who were they?"

"An American runner named Remo Black. Here is his picture. Very mean looking. The woman is named Littlefeather, something from a cowboy movie, I gather. She is a gymnast. They said they had gotten lost. They gave false names." He replaced the report on the pile. "They are not unusual. There are many like that. I'm worried about this." He pointed to the note from the S.A.A.E.

"A show of power," Bechenbauer repeated. "I wonder what that means."

The West German's face was grave and Sorkosfky knew he was reliving the horrors of Munich.

"Perhaps we will be lucky and not find out," the Rhino said.

The show of power was an explosion.

It was set off in a refreshment stand inside the village, early in the day, when there were no athletes nearby.

Jack Mullin, in Moscow as the director of the Baruban team, thought it best that no one be hurt by this blast. The way to create horror was insidiously, slowly, step by slow step, and deaths too early would work against his plan.

Mullin had one of his bogus Baruban athletes buy a soft drink at the stand and leave, conveniently forgetting his equipment bag. Mullin watched from a safe distance and when there was no one near the stand, he triggered the explosives with a small sending unit in his pocket. Then he walked away.

* * *

127

Remo and Chiun heard the explosion. They were in the stands of the stadium watching other runners practicing, getting the feel of the artificial cindered track that skirted the large field.

"An explosion," Remo said.

"You go," Chiun said. "I'm not interested." He had been sulking since Remo had carefully explained to him that he just simply could not disable all the athletes of the world so Remo could win all the gold medals.

"You'd better be interested," Remo said.

"I'm interested only in your gold medal, nothing else."

"Right. Because you want to get the credit and go on television and do commercials, right?"

"Something like that?"

"Well, Chiun, I'll tell you. If any athletes are killed here, the only television or press coverage is going to be of the killing. I won't even get my name in the paper. I won't be interviewed. I won't be anything, and that means you get nothing. So you'd better be interested."

"Why didn't you say so?" Chiun said. "Why are we sitting here wasting time talking?" He stood up and seemed to sniff the air like a bloodhound. "This way," he said and ran off toward the explosion.

The radio monitor on Sorkofsky's desk crackled, just as the Russian colonel and Bechenbauer were moving toward the door to investigate the sound of the explosion.

The report from one of the village security guards pinpointed the explosion at a refreshment stand.

"Anyone killed or hurt?" Sorkofsky asked over the radio.

"Unknown at this time, sir," the voice answered. Sorkofsky and Bechenbauer ran from the office.

* * *

Remo and Chiun brushed by the guards, who were trying to organize themselves without a commanding officer, and they had four minutes to pooch around in the rubble of the refreshment stand before they were ordered to leave.

The four minutes was enough.

Chiun picked up a small piece of heavy woven fabric from under the wood that had been the counter. He handed it to Remo who fingered it and said, "Probably an equipment bag."

Chiun nodded. "It would be reasonable. One could leave an equipment bag near a counter here without it being out of place. And what is unique about the bag?"

Remo looked again at the fabric as the security men herded them away from the ruins.

When they were back behind the police lines, Remo said, "Handwoven."

"Precisely," Chiun said. "But there is more."

They watched as a mammoth Russian officer, accompanied by a thin mustached man with the look of a ferret, arrived at the scene and began barking out orders. Instantly, the bombing scene began to take on some semblance of order. The big Russian was good, Remo thought to himself. He knew what to do and he knew how to command. There weren't many like that, either in the police or in the Army.

"Come," Chiun said. "What else?"

Remo turned and followed Chiun away from the scene. He did not notice the Russian officer look up and see him. The glint of recognition came over his eyes as he saw the face of Remo Black, which he had seen in that report on his desk earlier. Sorkofsky nodded to one of his plainclothes men, who came over to his side, listened to the colonel's whispered directions and then casually sauntered off in the direction Remo and Chiun had gone.

"I don't know, Chiun," said Remo, holding the

piece of cloth at arm's length for a different look. "What else?"

"Smell it," Chiun said.

Remo sniffed at the fabric, but could get only traces of aromas. He held the piece of cloth between his two hands tightly to warm it, inducing it to give off more of its scent, then raised his cupped hands to his nose and inhaled deeply.

There was the smoky burned smell, characteristic of explosive, but there was another smell too. It was bitterly sweet and pinched at his nostrils. Remo had smelled it before, a long time ago . . . but where?

He shook his head and tried again. He was able to pick out the scent now from among all the scents on the fabric—scents of gunpowder and sweat—but the sweet smell eluded him.

"I don't know, Chiun. What is it?"

"Arnica," Chiun said. "Smell it again, so you know it next time."

Remo sniffed it again and impressed the aroma on his memory.

"What's arnica?" he said.

"It comes from the dried flowers of an herb. It is made into an ointment and used by fighters to reduce swelling and cuts," Chiun said.

Remo remembered. It was back while he was in the army, long ago, long before CURE and long before Chiun, and he had been corraled into a boxing show. He had landed a lucky right hand and put a cut next to his opponent's eye, and in the next round, during a clinch, his nose was right next to the cut and he smelled the arnica that his opponent's corner had used to reduce the swelling and stop the flow of blood around the cut.

"A boxer," Remo said. "We're looking for a boxer."

"Yes," said Chiun. "And one from a country with handwoven bags."

130

Remo nodded. "Probably a small country that might be too poor for real equipment."

"Good," said Chiun. "I'm glad you understand. And now that I've done your work for you, I think I will return to the stadium and watch your opposition."

"All right," Remo said. "I'm going to the boxing arena. And I'll take the tail with me."

He nodded toward his own shoulder and Chiun nodded his understanding. Without even seeing the Russian agent, both had known they had been followed since leaving the refreshment stand.

Chiun strolled slowly back to the track and field arena stadium, while Remo walked off quickly toward the fieldhouse, where preliminary boxing bouts were starting. He would like to get this over quickly, he thought, so he could get to the other fieldhouse in time to watch Josie Littlefeather's routine on the balance beam.

In the boxing arena, Remo walked down the long corridor of dressing rooms, stopping into each one, wishing all the fighters good luck, and checking their equipment bags. His tail loitered in the corridor behind him, smoking and trying to look casual.

The last dressing room was labeled "People's Democratic Republic of Baruba," and as soon as Remo went in, he saw a woven equipment bag, its fabric identical to the shred of cloth in his hand, in a corner of the room near an open locker.

"Hey, pal," Remo said to the lone figure on the table. "Good luck." The black-skinned boxer looked up, startled, then responded to Remo's smile with a smile of his own.

"I hope you win today," Remo said. "What's your name?"

The black man hesitated a moment too long. "Sammy Wanenko" he said.

131

"Good," said Remo. "Well, good luck again." He shook the boxer's already-taped hand.

He wondered for a moment if he should shake the man up a bit and make him talk, but if he did, there would be questions and yap-yap and he would miss Josie's routine. He remembered the tail out in the hall. He would do to send the message back.

Remo went back into the corridor, and his tail pushed away from the wall where he had been lounging and lit a cigarette, his eyes watching the dark-haired American.

Remo beckoned to him.

"Come here," he said.

The Russian agent looked behind him, but there was nobody else in the corridor. He walked up to Remo, who grabbed the man's wrist, pulled him to the end of the corridor, and into a little alcove.

"You speak English?" Remo asked.

"Yes." The man was trying to free his wrist.

"Stop that," Remo said. "I just want to talk. I've got a message for your boss."

"Yes?"

"Tell him that the terrorists are the Baruban boxing team. You got that? The Baruban boxing team. Here. Give him this." He handed the agent the piece of woven fabric.

"This was at the scene of the bombing. It's how they planted the explosives," Remo said. "It's the material the Barubans use for their equipment bags. You got it?"

The Russian did not respond, but then quickly said "yes" when he felt something unbelievably hard probe his ribs right through the heavy suit he wore: Remo's index finger.

"Yes, yes," he said. "I got it."

"Okay. I've got to go. But you give him that message."

Remo took off on the run, to see Josie's routine.

132

The agent watched him leave, then looked at the fabric in his hands. Good old Colonel Sorkofsky, he thought. Trust the Rhino to spot somebody or something important.

He looked forward to hurrying back to Sorkofsky and giving him the American's information.

He walked back down the corridor, his eyes down, looking at the fabric in his hand.

He never heard the door of the Baruban dressing room open behind him, and it was too late when he heard the footstep behind him because a strong arm was already around his throat, and as he was being dragged into the dressing room, he saw the glint of a knife up over his head and then it felt like fire as it drove into his chest, tearing his heart muscle and making it stop.

CHAPTER THIRTEEN

"You did well," Flight Lieutenant Jack Mullin told the Baruban boxer.

The boxer was holding a white cloth to his bleeding forehead.

"I got knocked out in the first round," he said.

"I don't mean your bloody boxing match, you bleeding idiot," Mullin snarled. He pointed to the body of the dead Russian agent in a corner of the room. "I mean him."

The three other Africans masquerading as Baruban islanders nodded.

"Does anyone know who this American might be who talked to that agent?" Mullin asked.

One of the Africans said, "From the description, he sounds like the one called Remo Black. When I am at the track, he is all the Americans talk about. They say he is very strange."

"Probably CIA," said Mullin.

"His trainer is an Oriental," the African added. "Very old and frail. He wears nice robes. All sewn with pretty pictures and—"

"I'm not interested in his goddamn threads," Mullin said, and the African clamped his mouth shut in midsentence. "They will have to be taken care of. Both of them."

In a way, Mullin was glad that some pressure was building on his terrorist cadre. He was a man of action and the subterfuge and sneaking around was making him edgy. He could feel his blood beginning to pulse inside his temples.

He had another idea.

"The two security men. That big Russian and the German. If that American could find out something, perhaps they could too. I think we're going to leave our mark on these games, starting right now."

"What do you have in mind, Lieutenant?" asked one of the Africans.

"We are going to kill the security men. That should let the world know we mean business here."

He looked around the room at the four black faces. They all grinned back at him.

"This bomb was just the first step," Sorkofsky said. "We will have to act fast."

"What do you suggest?" Bechenbauer said.

"I think we will bring in this American." He lifted up the report with Remo's picture on it. "This Remo Black. He was at the scene; and yesterday he breached the village's security."

"You don't think he had anything to do with the bombing, do you? I can't believe a CIA man could be involved with this terrorist group."

"But he's not a CIA man," Sorkofsky said. "I just received a report from our central headquarters. They have means of checking personnel. He is not CIA. He is not FBI. He is not with any government agency."

"But still . . . an American going to bomb American athletes? I find that hard to believe," said the German.

"Listen," Sorkofsky said. "You know America is strange. They seem to delight in attacking their own country. Who knows what kind of a fishhead this one may be?"

He looked at Bechenbauer, who thought for a few long seconds, before nodding his agreement.

"I am going to have him picked up," Sorkofsky said.

As Sorkofsky reached for the phone, he was struck by the thought that he had promised to take his two daughters out for dinner that night in the city and then to the ballet. They would be bitterly disappointed, but once he had picked up this Remo Black, he would have to interrogate him to find out who he was working for. He would take the girls out to dinner tomorrow.

Bechenbauer found himself wishing that Remo Black *was* the head of the terrorists. He missed his wife and children, and he would be very happy to get home and see his family again.

Soon, he thought. *Perhaps very soon.*

Outside the security office, Mullin and his men had taken out the two Russian guards at the front door very smoothly and quietly, killing them with their knives. The door faced away from the heart of the Olympic village so there was little chance of their being spotted. Mullin posted one man as a lookout, while he worked on the locked door.

He felt the lock give and he turned to his men and whispered final instructions. "Remember. Quickly and quietly. I want no shooting, so hit them fast because as soon as they see us, they'll go for their guns. Understood?"

All of the men nodded. Then they heard the click of the lock as it opened.

Mullin could hear the blood pounding in his ears. This was what he lived for—action—and if action had to mean killing, so be it. He called to the lookout to join them. He held his knife in one hand and caressed the sharp blade with the other.

"All right, lads," he whispered. "In we go."

Sorkorfsky had just dialed the telephone when he saw the door fly open. Stunned, he watched as four black men and one white man flooded into the room and spread out in a fan shape. They were all armed with knives.

Bechenbauer saw the look on Sorkofsky's face and heard the door open behind him. He jumped out of his chair and turned to face whatever was coming. He did not have time to count the men who had entered the room and were charging them. He grabbed the chair he had been sitting in and threw it at one man, who ducked away from it. The chair struck him on the forearm and he heard the man cry out in pain or in anger.

With one hand frantically grabbing for his revolver, the West German felt the blade of the first knife cut into his flesh, below his belt, slicing his navel neatly in half. As that knife was pulled to the left, cutting him open at the belly, he felt a second blade rip into his throat and his cry of pain died there. He became very numb, very sleepy. His legs suddenly felt boneless and would not hold him. *I should be falling,* he thought, but instead he felt himself fading.

Soon, he thought, *soon. Soon . . . I . . . will . . . be . . . home . . .*

Sorkofsky could see Bechenbauer's back, but could not see what happened to him. Yet as the German slumped to the floor, he recognized what he had seen so many times before: the look of death. Pushing back his chair, the Russian put his feet against the edge of his desk and with all the power of his massive legs behind it, pushed out. The flimsy desk slid across the room, striking the already dead Bechenbauer in the back as he fell, but also sweeping one of the terrorists off his feet. That left four to deal with.

With the desk no longer protecting him, Sorkofsky jumped from his chair, his hand grabbing for the gun in the holster at his side. He was surprised at how calm he felt and how calculated his moves were. He knew exactly what he wanted to do and knew that if he could execute what he was planning, he had a chance to stay alive.

He had his gun in his hand and was raising it when the first knife found its mark.

One of the black men slashed at his gun arm, slicing it open just below the elbow. The hand went numb and he dropped the gun to the floor. At the same time, he grabbed the terrorist by the throat with his other hand and lifted him, like a toy, and threw him across the room where he crashed into another one of the Africans. Both went down in a tangled heap.

He looked down for his gun, but he saw a booted foot kick it away, then looked up and saw the small white man standing in front of him.

"You are a big lummox, aren't you?" said Mullin.

Sorkofsky did not understand the language, but the sneer on the white man's face and his sudden glimpse of poor Bechenbauer's body, bleeding on the floor, touched some deep nerve inside the Russian and he roared, a holler of anguish and pain from deep in his throat, and with his left hand he lashed out and grabbed the small Englishman's chin. He lifted him from the floor, with a strength born of pain and desperation, and charged across the floor, ready to slam the man's head into a wall. *I might die,* Sorkofsky thought *but this bastard will go with me.*

Mullin screamed and before Sorkofsky reached the far wall, two of the blacks tackled him. As he fell to the floor, he released Mullin. When he shook his head and cleared it, he saw the Englishman standing in front of him.

"On your feet, ox," the Englishman said. "I won't even need a knife for you."

His one arm useless, Sorkofsky rose to his feet. As he did, Mullin reached out and kicked the hard toe of a pointed boot into the Russian's solar plexus.

Sorkofsky, instead of going down, roared and charged at Mullin, but as he reached the small Englishman, Mullin twisted his knife upward into the Russian's stomach, and Dimitri Sorkofsky fell to the floor, his eyes already glazing over.

The room was as quiet as death.

"Well done, lads," Mullin said, although it was not as easy as he had anticipated or would have liked. The big Russian was a bloody bull and had made things more difficult than they should have been. Still, the terrorists' point had been made. The security officers for the Olympic Games were dead. The world would know the terrorists were not joking.

The telephone rang on the small phone ledge behind the spot where Sorkofsky's desk had stood.

Mullin said quickly, "All right, lads, let's go." As they went out the door, he added: "The American is next. This Remo Black."

CHAPTER FOURTEEN

Josie Littlefeather approached the balance beam for her third performance in the preliminaries and the crowd in the big gymnasium hushed.

Already she had done something no other American gymnast had ever done before: she had scored two perfect scores of ten in the preliminary competitions.

Remo nodded to himself with satisfaction as he saw her mount the bar with obvious assurance, and then with a physical happiness that bordered on lust, he watched her go through the turns and jumps and twists and somersaults of her routine, before leaving the bar with a twisting one-and-a-half-somersault dismount, that brought the crowd to its feet, roaring cheers of approval for the little-known American gymnast.

Josie ran to Remo and hugged him tightly.

"You were great," he said.

"Thanks to you," she said. As he looked over her shoulder, he saw the scores posted on the far side of the gymnasium. The audience erupted into more applause and cheering.

"Another ten?" she asked.

"Better believe it," Remo said. "Get out there and take a bow. Your audience is calling you."

Josie ran out onto one of the mats in the center of the floor and waved to the crowd, turning a slow circle, smiling honestly and brightly at the audience, and then she ran back over to join Remo on a bench near the spectators' seats.

"When do you compete?" she asked him.

He had not even thought about it. His first run was today too. In fact, they might even be looking for him. Missing the race now and disappointing Chiun would mean he would never hear the end of it.

Then he looked up and saw Chiun walking toward them, a grim look on his wizened face.

"Today," he said. "But don't come and watch. You'll only make me nervous."

She hugged him again and said, "Good luck, even though you don't need it. I have to go talk to somebody."

As she walked away, Remo rose to meet Chiun.

"It's okay, Chiun. It's okay. I won't miss the race."

"Did you find the bombers?" Chiun asked.

"Yeah. It's the Baruban team," Remo said.

"And you told the security chief of these games?"

"Not exactly."

"What not exactly?" asked Chiun.

"I told the guy who was tailing us. I told him to tell his boss."

"And then you came here so that you could watch that woman perform?"

"You've known about her," Remo said.

"How could I not know about her?" Chiun demanded. "The turmoil in your heart and head has made such a racket that I have not slept a wink since you met that woman. But she does not matter now."

"What does?"

"The security chiefs have been killed. I have just heard," Chiun said. "I guess your message about the terrorists was not delivered."

"Damn," snapped Remo. He felt responsible and he felt bad. He had been responsible for the death of many men, but this was from negligence, not by design.

He looked up at Chiun. "Let's go get those damned terrorists and put them out of action for good."

Chiun raised his hand. "No. *I* will go and find them. You will do what you came here to do. Get over to the sports field and win your race. Put all else out of your mind until you win."

"Chiun—"

"Shhh. This is important. You go win. This is not for the gold medal yet. It is just a preliminary. But you win it. And set a new world's record while you're doing it. Not a big world's record, but just a little one. Save the good stuff for later. But remember. Don't go on television until I get back. That is important, because you will probably say all the wrong things. Do what I tell you."

"Yes, Chiun," Remo said, and the two men walked off in separate directions, Chiun to hunt, and Remo to run.

The event was the 800-meter run.

Remo arrived barely in time to avoid being disqualified and was glared at malevolently by three other American runners.

Remo debated whether or not he should wave at Dr. Harold W. Smith, who was probably watching at home, but decided against it. Smith probably already had apoplexy from seeing Josie Littlefeather run over after her balance beam performance and hug Remo.

Remo was still wearing chinos and loafers. One of the field judges said to him, "Where is your uniform?"

"This is it," Remo said. "I'm representing the Tool and Die Makers Athletic Club of Secaucus, New Jersey."

The judge shook his head in disbelief and stepped away from the starting line.

Remo was in lane four, next to the east German runner, Hans Schlichter, who had seen Remo in the gymnasium showing Josie how to master the balance beam. The East German leaned over to him and said, "It is nothing personal, you understand."

"Of course," said Remo. "Just in the spirit of Olympic competition."

"That is right," said Schlichter.

The runners took their place in the starting blocks, except for Remo who chose to stand at the start line.

When the gun sounded, Schlichter, instead of exploding from the blocks, swerved out to the right. This made room for another East German runner to move inside, past Schlichter and alongside Remo, pinching the American between himself and another East German runner on Remo's left.

Remo started slowly down the track, and the two East German runners kept swerving in and out of their lines, bumping him, pinching him between them. One tried on a forward stride to dig his running spikes into Remo's right calf, but Remo dodged.

Up ahead, he saw Hans Schlichter racing into a large lead, and as Schlichter cut over toward the rail, he glanced back at Remo and the look on his face said clearly, "Sorry, pal, but that's the way it is."

And Remo got angry.

He started running in an exaggerated motion, swinging his arms up and forward, and then he brought his left elbow back into the midsection of one East German runner who gasped out his air. Remo's right fist slapped downward and hit into the left thigh of the runner on his right, and the runner shouted his pain, slowed up, and then tried to run off the pain. But it was too late. Remo was past them, chasing Schlichter and the three Americans who held

147

second, third and fourth places behind the East German star.

As he ran, Remo shook his head. *What ever happened to sportsmanship?* he asked himself, and he put out of his mind the necessity of winning the race and gave himself just one goal: get rid of that East German sucker.

Running easily now, Remo came up behind the three American runners halfway through the second and last lap of the race.

The crowd began to roar as Remo moved past the three Americans. Schlichter thought it was for him, until he saw Remo pull up alongside him. His eyes widened and he tried to turn on some extra energy to leave Remo behind him, but Remo stayed right with him effortlessly.

"Communists suck," Remo said.

Schlichter kept running.

"You look like Hitler. You related?" Remo said.

Schlichter glanced angrily to his right, his face beaming hatred at Remo.

They were near the backstretch now and the smooth stride of Schlichter started to get choppy. Remo felt the three American runners closing behind them.

"Your mother still turning tricks at the Berlin Wall?" Remo asked Schlichter as he matched him, easy stride for tortured stride.

Schlichter turned to Remo and hissed, "You are a Yankee bastard."

"Crap," Remo said. *"Ich bin ein Berliner.* You're a schmuck."

Schlichter tried to concentrate on his running, but the three Americans now were running alongside them.

"A running dog of the Communist butchers," Remo said. "Remember Hungary. Remember Czechoslovakia. Free Poland."

148

And incredibly, Schlichter stopped running and jumped toward Remo, flailing punches at him. Remo ducked and trotted off from the East German, watching the three Americans cross the finish line ahead of him almost shoulder to shoulder, and it was only when the roar from the crowd signalled that the race was over that he realized he had blown it and would have to face Chiun.

Behind him, Schlichter did not even bother to finish the race. He stopped and walked off the track, joined by the other two East Germans, all eliminated in the competition's first heat. They looked toward Remo and he tossed them a salute.

He congratulated the three successful Americans, and one of them threw his arms around Remo.

"You cooked him good, pal. You could have won this thing, don't think we don't know that. But why?"

"Ah, you guys deserve it." Remo said. "Besides, you're getting old. This is your last shot. I'll be back in four years and maybe I'll even buy a pair of sneakers and blow everybody out." The three runners, all fifteen years younger than Remo, laughed.

"Yeah, but we'll get medals this year. What'll you get?"

"Satisfaction," Remo said. "That's all I wanted."

He turned and saw Josie Littlefeather standing in the crowd of people who had spilled onto the track. He could see hurt in her eyes, and he was sad that he had disappointed her by losing, but even that could not make him regret what he had done.

He walked toward her, calling her name: "Josie." She turned away, blindly plunging through the crowd and quickly becoming lost.

"Josie," he called again, but she did not stop.

His first thought was that she would get over it. His second thought was to hell with her if she didn't.

Then he remembered that while he was standing

there, thinking about his running antics, Chiun was out hunting killers.

And damn him, Remo thought, *he'd better save me something.*

CHAPTER FIFTEEN

The center of the Olympic village was filled with tourists and athletes, strolling from arena to arena, gymnasium to gymnasium, but Jack Mullin did not see them. What he saw instead was hundreds of policemen and soldiers, moving through the crowd, scanning faces, as if looking for someone.

He became nervous. He pulled his four men close to him and said, "I think, lads, it's time to plant our little packages and get out. Agreed?"

He scanned their impassive faces. Not a muscle moved in any of them.

"Too many police. So we'll do what we have to do. You plant your little gifts where we decided and I'll keep looking for the American. When you're done, we'll meet in the back of the big hall where they're holding the weight-lifting competition. Get on with you, now."

The four men scurried off and Mullin turned to continue his search for Remo.

So things were a little ahead of schedule, but so what. That was what made a good commander, Mullin knew, the ability to adapt plans to actual conditions. Plans were fine, but they could work to the letter only in a hermetically sealed world and he didn't live in one of those.

He wondered where Remo might be. He had missed him at the running track. But he'd find him and kill him, and that would be that. He and his men would be on their way back home, and if everything went the way it should, the Jimbobwu Mkombu revolution should get a big leg up on toppling the governments of Rhodesia and South Africa.

And then Jack Mullin would topple Mkombu. *Not too long now,* he thought. But first the American, Remo Black, and the old Oriental.

The four bogus Baruban athletes were walking through the crowded village with their equipment bags of explosives.

And then there were three.

The African who had impersonated Sammy Wanenko, the Baruban boxer, felt a hand around the back of his neck. He wanted to call out to his companions to stop, but no sound would come. When the hand lightened its grip, he turned and saw standing before him a small, aged Oriental.

"Where is your leader?" Chiun asked.

"Who wants to know, old man?"

Chiun explained who he was by slapping his right hand to the side of the African's cheek. Nothing he had felt that day in the ring while he was on his brief way to a first round knockout had felt like that. His face felt aflame; he could almost hear the skin bubbling and sputtering where the old man had slapped it.

Then Chiun was in close to him, his left hand buried in the African's belly, and the African was babbling about Lieutenant Mullin, and what he looked like, and where he was going, and how his target was Remo Black, and how his three companions were on their way to set bombs in the American athletes' dormitories, and then the African died in a lump on the village pavement.

Chiun walked away from the body. Should he go after the three Africans with the bombs? Or after Jack Mullin? He decided on Mullin. The athletes' dormitories were empty now and would be for some time; there would be no danger for a while. But Mullin could be dangerous to Remo, particularly if Chiun's young disciple was still wandering around with his head in the clouds, mooning over that Indian woman.

He saw Mullin outside the entrance to one of the gymnasium buildings and Chiun moved through the outskirts of the crowd, until he came to view in front of Mullin. He kept his back to the Englishman, so that the Englishman could think that he had found Chiun on his own.

Mullin saw the brocaded robe on the tiny Oriental with his back to him.

"Hey, old boy," he called.

Chiun turned and stared at Mullin. His face was expressionless. Mullin slipped a knife from his pocket, held it to Chiun's belly, and said: "Move alongside the building." They were in an alley with large dump containers of garbage. Mullin herded Chiun along and the old man obeyed, still without expression. *No wonder they called Orientals inscrutable,* Mullin thought.

When they were out of sight of the crowd, Mullin said, "Where's the American?"

Chiun was silent.

"C'mon, you blasted old chink, where is he?"

Still no answer. Mullin sighed and slashed with his knife to take out the old man's throat.

He missed.

That was impossible.

He slashed again.

Again he missed.

Bloody impossible. The old fool was standing right there. He hadn't even moved. How could he miss?

Or had he moved?

Mullin slashed at him again, but watched very closely. He caught just a faint whisper of a move-

154

ment, as if in a fraction of a second the old man had withdrawn from the path of the knife and then slid back to his original position.

Mullin put the knife back into its pocket sheath and pulled his .45 out from under his bush jacket. Time to stop fooling around.

"Okay, old man. One last time. Where is the American?"

Silence.

Mullin pulled the trigger. The shot exploded in the alley with a booming crack.

And missed.

"Damn it," Mullin snapped. How could he have missed? The old man couldn't duck a bullet. Could he?

He fired another shot. The old man just stood there, unharmed.

Mullin looked at his gun as if it were the gun's fault, then back at the old man.

Inscrutable? No. Inhuman was more like it.

Mullin felt a twinge of an emotion he was not used to: fear.

He was not in control of himself as he backed away, slowly at first, then faster, until he was almost running, all the while hearing his mind berate him for running from a scrawny old man.

But this was not a normal old man.

Chiun smiled as he followed. He had succeeded in persuading Mullin to give up the search for Remo and to join the other terrorists. Now Chiun could round them up and hold them for Remo, who would want to ask questions and do many other silly things, but Chiun would forgive them all today because after all Remo was going to win him a gold medal.

He hoped that Remo did not win his race by running at top speed. He wanted Remo to break the world's record bit by bit through the preliminaries and then shatter it in the final race for the Olympic gold.

Mullin ran at top speed. He was trying to think of some reasonable explanation for what had happened. He was also trying to regain control of his body, which was continuing to rush forward, even as his mind commanded it to slow down. This feeling, this panicky flight from a frail old Chinaman, was totally alien to Jack Mullin. Gradually, he got his body back under control, talking away the fear. *Once I join up with my other four men,* he told himself, *we'll take care of the Chink and the American.*

He checked his watch. The explosive charges should be set by now and his men should be waiting for him at the back of the main hall, where the weightlifting was being held.

He was walking now and felt back in control . . . of everything but his neck.

He could not quite get it to let his head turn around to take a look behind him.

Remo pushed through the crowd in the village, hoping mostly that he could find Chiun and partially that he would never see him again so that he did not have to tell him about this afternoon's race which had eliminated Remo from Olympic competition.

From the corner of his eye, he caught a glimpse of flashing blue disappearing into the main hall. He knew it was Chiun's brocaded blue robe.

He followed.

Alexi Vassilev put powder on the inside of his massive thighs as the Russian coach told him, "You are the greatest, Alexi. The greatest that ever was."

Vassilev grunted. His grunt would be enough to knock some men over. He was six-foot-three and weighed 345 pounds, and for two successive Olym-

156

pics he had been the superheavyweight weightlifting champion of the world.

But today he was worried. He was thirty-eight years old and the pulled muscles and the hyper-extended tendons and ligaments no longer healed as quickly as they once did, and also he felt on his neck the hot breath of a world of lifters who had come finally to realize that Vassilev was human and might, just might, be beaten.

In the past he had disdained setting world's records. He owned every record in the world, but he never tried to lift for a record. He had always lifted only enough to win.

But today, at thirty-eight and nervous, he was going to lift a record. He was going to set a mark that would intimidate generations of weight-lifters and would guarantee that even when his aging body gave out and he lost a competition, his government would not respond as they had with so many failed athletes in the past, by taking away their apartment and their car and shipping them off to live someplace where man could not live. They would continue to honor his record.

There was a saying among the athletes on the Olympic Russian team, "Training is hard, but so is Siberian ice."

His coach kept babbling. "You are the greatest, Alexi. The greatest." Vassilev nodded but he was not listening.

His primary opponent today would be an American lifter who had won a television competition as "Mister Strongman," which title he earned by carrying a refrigerator up a hill. That this task was accomplished every day by dozens of moving men in the city of San Francisco seemed to have been lost on the judges.

But despite his bogus credentials, the American was a good lifter, Vassilev realized.

"I must win," he mumbled aloud.

"Of course you win," said his coach.

"This will be my last Olympics," he said. "I crush that American today. I will show the glory of Soviet Socialist Republics."

He looked at his coach carefully, making sure that the man had caught his words properly so he could report them back to the secret police which kept a close eye on an athlete's actions and words.

"You will win for Mother Russia," his coach said.

And for me, Vassilev thought.

It was time.

He walked out onto the platform to thunderous applause. His face was stolid, unmoving, and he characteristically ignored the audience, concentrating solely on the weight before him. It was loaded with 600 pounds and the crowd hummed with anticipation. Vassilev was going to try to jerk 600 pounds, for in excess of anything anyone had ever lifted before. It was the equivalent of a three-minute mile.

Breathing deeply, rhythmically, Vassilev bent down and placed his hands on the cold bar, flexing his fingers around it for the right grip, finally grabbing it tightly. With one explosive gasp of air he brought the weight to his chest.

He took a deep breath. He felt his hands sweating and he knew it was time to jerk the bar overhead before it slipped. He blew out the air, pushed the weight up over his head, but before he could lock his elbows to hold it in place, it slid from his damp hands and hit the wooden platform in front of him with a crashing thud.

Vassilev cursed inwardly. He had failed on the first of three lifts.

The relief that Mullin had felt when he spotted the main hall had annoyed him. It was a disgrace, he thought, that a soldier who had been decorated in

Her Majesty's Air Force was running from an old man, trying to join up with four blackamoor toy soldiers, and feeling relief that he had almost reached them.

He was ashamed of himself. It was all that Chinaman's fault.

He stopped at the door to the hall and cursed out loud, wishing for a moment that something would will him to go back and take that Chinaman on alone, this time hand to hand, and cut him into bits. But no voice inside him said to do that and so he opened the door and walked inside the great hall, looking around in the back for his men. He did not see them.

On the platform, he recognized the strongest man in the world, Alexi Vassilev. With his great potbelly, the center of gravity that was so valuable to weightlifters, Vassilev had hoisted weights no other man was capable of, *and yet,* Mullin thought, *I could defeat him hand to hand with no problem.* And still . . . a scrawny old Chinaman . . .

He walked around the back of the hall, behind the crowd. Suddenly he heard the gasp and the sound of the weight hitting the platform. He looked up to see Vassilev with a look of pain on his face, after failing to hold the weight.

That's okay, Alexi, he thought. *We all have our bad days. You and I are the best but we're just having a bad day.*

He felt better suddenly. A bad day, that's all it was. Maybe even just a bad moment.

Sure.

And with that thought, he was able to turn his neck and take a look behind him.

What he saw made his blood go cold. That damned Chinaman. He was standing just inside the door, staring at Mullin with those cold hazel eyes.

"Damn you," Mullin shouted, but nobody heard

because Vassilev was again approaching the weight.

Mullin ran.

Vassilev was going to try again. This was his last chance, his third attempt. His coach wanted him to rest before trying another lift, but he waved his handler away and simply walked around the weight and began to stare straight ahead, into space, over the heads of the audience.

Get it over with, he told himself. *Do it now. Win or lose now.*

His hands were sweating and for the first time in many years, he felt the pinch of nervousness in his stomach as he bent over and placed his hands around the cold textured steel of the bar.

Mullin ran down the left side of the hall, toward the stage, and the back door leading outside. The crowd was dense and there was no way for Chiun to get through without hurting someone. He ran down the right side of the building. He saw Mullin slip through a back door to go outside.

There was only one way to follow him: Across the weight-lifters' platform.

Remo entered just as Chiun hopped up onto the platform. He watched as Chiun stopped before a thick television cable that crisscrossed back and forth, barring his path. Chiun grasped the cable in his two small hands and ripped the inch-thick strands cleanly in half.

Sparks flew. TV technicians shouted. Chiun ignored them and started across the platform just as Alexi Vassilev hoisted the 600-pound barbell to his chest.

Vassilev felt a rush of relief as he took a deep breath, exploded it outward, and hoisted the weight overhead. He locked his elbows and held the weight.

How foolish he had been to be nervous. Who but the great Vassilev could ever lift such a weight and hold it with such ease?

The audience exploded with cheers, and Vassilev gave them a rare small smile, but he waited for the judges to signal that he had held the weight long enough for the lift to count. Then he saw the audience's eyes move off him. He looked toward his right, toward where all the people were looking, and saw a blue-robed Oriental running across the platform.

Staggering under the weight, still awaiting the judges' signal, Vassilev stumbled two steps forward in the Oriental's path. How dare this little man detract from Alexi's great moment?

He was standing right in the Oriental's way.

"How dare you?" he bellowed in Russian.

He could not believe what happened and the next day in the hospital he would not be able to explain.

He heard the Oriental say in perfect Russian, "Out of my way, gross meat-eater," and then he was being lifted up—he and the great 600 pounds he held—they were being effortlessly lifted by this frail old Oriental, who tossed them both through the air toward the rear of the platform, and then continued to run off the stage, as the audience sat in shocked silence.

Remo watched in amusement as Chiun hoisted the thousand pounds of Vassilev and steel and threw them out of his way as if they weighed no more than a child's slipper.

The weight slipped from Vassilev's hands as he sailed through the air, so the two did not land together. Remo was hard put to figure out which of the two bounced higher, but Vassilev remained stationary and the weight hit and rolled.

Remo ran down the left side of the hall and met Chiun at the rear door.

When Jack Mullin had run outside, he had found his men waiting for him. Only three, not four, and the fools as usual had misunderstood his instructions. He had told them to meet him in the back of the hall. They had interpreted that to mean they should meet him in back of the hall. He would skin them for that one day.

They ran toward him as he came out into the bright sun. They were all armed with handguns.

"The Oriental will be coming through that door in a moment," he explained. "Cut him down when he does. All the explosives are planted?"

"Yes, Lieutenant."

The four men aimed their automatics at the door. Mullin felt his palms sweaty and slick. Perspiration was also flowing down his forehead and dripping from his eyebrows.

C'mon, Mullin mumbled toward the closed door. *Get out here and get it over with.*

"They are probably outside waiting," Chiun told Remo.

"So what?" Remo asked.

"If they fire, the bullets might hit somebody in here. Smith would not like that," Chiun said.

Remo thought of that for a moment, then nodded.

"All right. Then up we go."

He grabbed hold of a rope that led to a second-floor window and raced up it, like a trained monkey, climbing with just his hands, feeling behind him the speed of Chiun following him.

"Where is he, Lieutenant?" one of Mullin's men asked.

162

"He's coming through that door," Mullin said. "There's no other way."

"No?" said Remo from behind Mullin and as the Briton turned, Remo said, "Surprise. Surprise."

When Mullin saw Chiun standing next to Remo, his control snapped.

"Kill them. Kill them," he screamed.

The four men leveled their automatics at Remo and Chiun, but before they could squeeze triggers, Remo and Chiun were among them and bullets could not be fired without risking hitting one of their own men. The four terrorists pulled their knives from their belts.

Or three of them did. One had the knife in his hand and his hand on the way up, when his wrist collided with the side of Chiun's hand, flailing downward in the classical hand-ax position. The knife went clattering one way; the hand bounced off in another direction; and the terrorist, looking down at the bleeding stump of his wrist, fell backwards into a sitting position on the hard pavement.

"How much did you win by?" Chiun called over his shoulder.

"What?" Remo asked. He had moved inside one of the terrorist's knives, continued past him, then slammed back with his right elbow into the man's right kidney. Before the man could fall, Remo had the body under the armpits.

Chiun said, "You heard my question. How much did you win by?"

Remo lifted the body and swung it out at a third terrorist who slid back out of range.

"Actually, Chiun, I didn't win," Remo said, moving forward on the third terrorist.

Chiun was moving in on Jack Mullin. He stopped and turned to Remo, hands on his hips, his hazel eyes narrowed until they were mere slits in his parchment-yellow face.

"Explain yourself," he demanded.

"Chiun, I'm a little busy," Remo said, as he threw the dead terrorist in his arms at the third terrorist. The weight crashed the man to the ground.

"Nonsense, busy," Chiun said. "You stop fooling around with those creatures and talk to me."

Remo turned toward Chiun. The third African, carried to the ground by the weight of his dead partner, extricated himself, rolled to his belly and aimed his automatic at Remo's stomach.

"You lost," Chiun accused.

"Let me explain," Remo said.

"You lost deliberately."

"For a good reason, Chiun."

"There is no good reason for a Master of Sinanju, even such a worthless one as you, to lose. That is without honor."

Just as the third terrorist squeezed the trigger, Remo, without turning, kicked out with his left foot and buried his shoe into the man's skull, in the thin spot between the eyes. The brain no longer ordered the finger to squeeze the trigger and both man and gun clattered onto the ground.

That left Jack Mullin.

"Losing today was a matter of honor, Chiun," Remo said. He was glancing at Mullin, who was backing away from the two men, trying to get far enough from them, so he could be sure to take them both out with bullets from his .45.

"All that training wasted by an ingrate, a white ingrate, a dead-white-like-a-dead-fish-pale-piece-of-pig's-ear-ingrate."

"Dammit, Chiun," said Remo.

"C'mon," Mullin yelled. He was fifteen feet from them now. His eyes were rolling wildly in his head. He pointed the automatic at first Chiun, then Remo. "C'mon," he yelled. "I'll get you. I'll take you both."

"You be quiet," Chiun said. "I'm not ready to deal with you yet. First this ingrate."

"I know that gold medal meant a lot to you, Chiun. You've got to believe I didn't just lose it on a whim."

Chiun was disgusted. He threw his hands in the air in exasperation, turned, and walked away from Remo and Mullin. The Englishman carefully aimed his automatic at Chiun's thin back.

This time, he would not miss. This time, that old man was his. *Let's see how inscrutable he'll be when he's dead,* Mullin thought.

He forgot Remo and as his finger tightened on the trigger, he felt the gun slapped from his hands and saw it bounce away along the thin blacktop pavement.

"Aaaaaaarghhhhhh," screamed Mullin, his voice quivering in anguish.

"Where'd you plant the bombs?" Remo asked.

"Find them yourself," Mullin said. Remo buried his hand in Mullin's left side and the Englishman screamed in pain.

"The bombs," said Remo.

"Around the American barracks," Mullin said.

"So long, Major Blimp," said Remo, and he slowly removed his hand from Mullin's left side and Mullin felt a flash of cool air there and realized that his side had been opened and his vital organs exposed, but before he could wonder how Remo had done that without a knife, he fell dead to the ground.

Remo wiped his hand on Mullin's shirt. Forty yards away, Chiun was still marching resolutely off.

"I saved your life," Remo yelled. "I really did. He was going to shoot you and I saved you."

And Chiun's voice wafted back toward Remo.

"Blow it out your ears," called the Master of Sinanju.

CHAPTER SIXTEEN

It was the next-to-the-last day of competition. The bombs had been removed from the American athletes' quarters without incident. The Russian secret police had announced that they had apprehended the terrorists, but refused to give details beyond their announcement that "again the forces of reactionary racist capitalist imperialism had succumbed to the superior intelligence and dedication of the Soviet socialist system."

And Remo had not spoken to Josie Littlefeather since the day he had lost his race.

But he was sitting near the bench as her competition was slowly winding down to its final day. Josie had continued to stun the crowd by scoring nothing but tens on the balance beam. She was far ahead in that contest, and her score on the beam had kept her respectably close with an outside chance for a silver medal in the overall gymnastic competition.

Remo watched as Josie applied rosin to her hands and approached the beam. She mounted it cleanly and performed brilliantly, and Remo saw, by the confidence with which she moved, that the imaginary red line down the center of the imaginary wide wooden bar was still there in her mind.

Her dismount was perfect. So was her score. All tens. Just one more day to go for the gold.

As she came off the floor, she was surrounded by

reporters who wanted to talk to her. Remo saw someone in the crowd pushing the reporters back, making room for her. His stomach fell when he saw who it was. Vincent Josephs, the sports agent, who had wanted to sign up Remo and manage his career.

Remo saw Josephs walk toward the arena exit and the press tent. Josie Littlefeather followed him, ignoring the questions of the trailing pack of reporters.

Remo tagged along. He wanted to hear her tell her story about how winning the gold medal would bring pride to her tribe of Blackhand Indians.

When Remo entered the tent, he almost bumped into Vincent Josephs, who was checking to make sure that all the major press outlets were represented.

"Stand in the back, kid, and don't talk," he told Remo. "This tent is for winners."

"She hasn't won yet," Remo said.

"It's a chip shot," Vincent Josephs said. "Tomorrow is a breeze."

Josie saw Remo standing in the back of the tent and when his eyes met hers, she quickly looked away. With Josephs at her side, she began to field the reporters' questions. She remembered all the answers she had been taught.

Her uniform, made by Lady Bountiful, fit perfectly and gave her the freedom for her championship performance.

She owed her conditioning to Krisp-and-Lite breakfast cereal, which she had eaten every day since childhood.

She protected herself against slipping by using Shur-Fire Rosin, the stickum of champions, and when she wasn't competing, she liked to rest around the wigwam in her perfectly comfortable, warming Hotsy Totsy Slippers by Benningham Mills, made of the new wonder knit, More-on.

She never mentioned Remo, which did not hurt his

169

feelings. She never once mentioned winning the medal for the Blackhand Indians, which did hurt Remo's feelings.

Remo waited by the entrance to the tent so Josie would have to pass by him when they left. Reporters wanted her to come outside, and do a couple of handstands and cartwheels for publicity photos. She would be America's first woman gymnast gold medalist in history. The only way she could lose tomorroe would be to fall off the bar and stay off.

He blocked Josie's way as she came toward the tent entrance.

"Congratulations," he said. "I'm sure all the folks back home on the reservation will be proud of you, even if you did forget to mention them."

She tossed her long hair back over her shoulder and stared at him, as if he were an autograph hound bothering her in a restroom.

"You were right," she said, "when you said that if I could work my way off the reservation, so could they. I have an opportunity now with Mr. Josephs to make a name for myself."

"And a lot of money," Remo said.

"Right. And a lot of money and there's no law against it. Maybe I'll see you around, Remo. Now, the photographers are waiting."

Vincent Josephs went ahead of her and as she passed Remo he reached out and delicately touched her lower back.

She turned. "What was that for?" she asked. She felt strangely uncomfortable. She knew he'd only touched her lightly, but for some reason she could still feel it and it seemed to be spreading through her body.

"You'll never forget that touch, Josie," said Remo. "It's very special. Any time you try to perform any kind of gymnastic move, you'll remember that touch. When you mount a balance beam, you'll think of it,

170

and when you do, you'll think about that beam and you're going to know it's not two feet wide with a red stripe down the middle. You're going to remember that it's only a piece of wood, four inches wide, and every time you try to climb on it, you're going to fall off, right on your lovely ass."

She frowned at him. "You're crazy," she told him, not wanting to believe it.

Suddenly, Vincent Josephs was back.

"Hey, honey, come on outside. They want some pictures, you know, handstands and flips and stuff. C'mon, let's go tantalize them . . . champ."

She hesitated.

"Go ahead, Josie," said Remo, with a cold smile. "Go do a few flips and handstands for them. And for me and the folks back home."

Josephs grabbed her arm and pulled her out of the tent and Remo walked out behind them, then turned and walked away.

Behind him, he heard the photographers laugh. He turned to watch.

Josie tried a handstand and lost her balance and fell over.

The photographers chuckled and Vincent Josephs laughed it off.

"Just nerves, fellas. Come on, Josie, put on a show for the boys."

She looked up and her eyes met Remo's. She looked apprehensive.

She tried to do a cartwheel, a children's exercise in a schoolyard, and fell heavily to the ground.

The photographers laughed and Remo walked away, back toward the room which he and Chiun would soon leave for a plane to London.

CHAPTER SEVENTEEN

In the fifth floor room at London's Dorchester Arms, Smith was trying to talk, but Chiun sat silently in the middle of the floor, arms folded, eyes staring into eternity, and Remo was watching the women's gymnastic competition on television.

"So it has ended reasonably well," Smith said. "The explosives were all removed, and the Russians have decided not to protest against our obviously having sneaked some agents into the games without their permission."

He got the feeling he was talking into an empty cave. Chiun did not move, not even so much as flickering an eyelid. Remo remained glued to the television set. An announcer, presumably chosen for hyperthyroidism, was shouting: "Now, here's the surprise star of the games. Josie Littlefeather. This little red woman hasn't been anything but perfect since she first set foot on the balance beam here in Moscow. All tens."

And horning in on his voice was the voice of a young woman commentator who was herself an ex-athlete but tended to forget it in the flood of gee-whizzes and wows which made up her broadcasting vocabulary. "That's right, folks," she said, "and, gee whiz, all Josie's got to do right now is score an eight and she's got this balance beam competition all locked up."

"Scoring an eight shouldn't be hard, should it?" said the male commentator.

"All you've got to do is stay on the beam and you'll get an eight," the girl said.

"Yeah?" snarled Remo to the television set. "Watch this."

Smith shook his head. Both Remo and Chiun had been acting strangely since they returned last night from Moscow. He leaned over on his couch seat to look over Remo's shoulder at the television set. He saw an Indian girl with her hair tied up in a bun apply rosin to her hands, then move to the balance beam, put her hands on it, and lift herself up to the narrow plank of wood. Then her hands seemed to slip, and she fell to the matting surrounding the beam.

"Way to go, Josie," shouted Remo.

The girl leaped back up to the beam, but her foot slipped and she landed heavily on her backside. She grabbed the beam desperately to stop herself from falling off.

"Swell, sweetheart," Remo said.

Finally she raised herself to a standing position on the beam. She took a step forward, planted her right foot, tried to do a forward walkover, but her left foot slipped and she fell off the beam onto the mat.

"She's blowing it," the young woman commentator said. "Wow, folks, Josie had it all in her hands and she's blowing it."

"I guess she's blowing it," said the male announcer, not to be outdone in technical analysis.

Josie Littlefeather got up quickly and made one last attempt to mount the beam, but as her feet hit it, they slid out from under her and she fell to her backside, then rolled off onto the mat, then got up and ran off the floor, out of the arena. She was rubbing her back.

175

"Yaaaaay," yelled Remo. He stood up and kicked off the television with his toe. He turned to Smith. "You were saying?"

"Why were you cheering that poor girl's disaster?" Smith asked.

"Just collecting a due bill," Remo said. "What about the Russians?"

"They are not going to complain that our country sent some agents into the games without their permission."

"That's big of them," Remo said. "They got all the bombs out?"

"Yes. They were in the ventilation shafts in each of the building's wings. It would have been a disaster."

"Good," Remo said. "And who were the terrorists?"

Smith dug in his attaché case and brought out a photo, which he handed to Remo. "I think it was him."

Remo looked at him. "I thought Idi Amin had been disposed of."

"That's not Idi Amin. That's Jimbobwu Mkombu."

"Who's he?"

"He leads one of the terrorist armies that have been trying to overthrow the governments of South Africa and Rhodesia."

Remo nodded. "I got it. Make it look like the South African whites were trying to upset the Olympics and kill American athletes. Get the world ticked off at them, and then move in and take over."

"That's about it," Smith said.

"What's going to happen to him?"

"Nothing," said Smith. "In the first place, we can't be 100 percent sure that he sent this Lieutenant Mullin and the other four men to disrupt the games."

"He sent them," Remo said.

"I think so too, because Mullin had been working for him for three years. But we can't prove it."

"What about the Russians?" asked Remo.

"Well, they've been supporting Mkombu's revolution. They're not about to announce that one of their own tried to mess up their games. That's why they're not announcing the identity of the terrorists."

"So Mkombu's going to get away with it," Remo said.

Smith shrugged. "Apparently. He might even get some good out of it for himself. Without any contradiction, much of the world is still going to believe it was the whites in Southern Africa who tried to blow up the games. That might strengthen Mkombu's hand."

"That's not fair," Remo said.

"Hah," said Chiun. "A fitting end to these games, then. Nothing is fair."

He continued to look straight ahead and Smith looked toward Remo for an explanation.

"He's ticked 'cause I didn't win a medal," Remo said.

"Nothing has gone right in these Olympics," Chiun said. "Nothing has happened the way I planned."

The self-pity oozed from his voice and Remo wondered if he should tell Smith what had happened. Yesterday, returning from Moscow, Chiun had become philosophical about Remo's defeat, and when Remo had pressed him, he found out that Chiun had figured out a new way to gain fame and fortune from the games. Chiun had decided that the entire world saw him lift Vassilev and the six hundred pounds of weights and this should bring the offers of endorsement contracts to him immediately in great floods. It was only when they reached London that Chiun found out that the television had blacked out at just that moment, and no one had seen him toss Vassilev around like a rag doll. Remo had not had the heart to tell Chiun that it was Chiun's own fault: that when he snapped the television cable that was blocking his way, he had stopped the TV transmission of the weight-lifting competition.

"I'm sorry for that, Chiun," Smith said.

Chiun eyed the ceiling in disgust, and Remo felt sorry for him. Chiun had not gotten his gold medal, had missed out on all his endorsement contracts, and had experienced nothing but disappointment because of Jimbobwu Mkombu. And Mkombu might turn the entire thing into a great success for himself.

That wasn't fair, Remo decided.

"So Mkombu's going to get away with it," he said to Smith.

"Probably."

"Maybe," said Remo.

At that moment, he decided the job was not yet done.

CHAPTER EIGHTEEN

Carried by jungle drums, passed in whispered word from one soldier to another, the story spread through the jungles above South Africa and Rhodesia that a slim white avenger stalked the jungles, seeking vengeance.

The stories said he was able to move unbelievably fast; that he was there one moment and gone the next. That bullets could not hurt him. That he smiled when he killed—smiled and spoke of vengeance for the sake of honor.

And Jimbobwu Mkombu's soldiers worried, because the trail of bodies was coming through the jungles toward them. And the soldiers asked themselves, "Why should we die this way for him? On a battlefield, yes, because we are soldiers, but at the hands of a white avenging spirit who smiles when he kills? That is no way for soldiers to die."

"He wants the general," one soldier told another. "Why should we die in his place?"

The other soldier heard a noise and fired a shot into the brush. Both men listened, but heard nothing.

"Do not let the general hear you speak that way," the second soldier warned. "He would have you shot or have your head torn off. He is very nervous these days."

"Of course. He knows this white avenger is coming for him."

"Silence, you fools," roared Mkombu's voice from

180

above their heads. "How can I hear what is going on in the jungle if you keep whispering and mumbling? Be quiet, you dogs."

The first man leaned over to the second soldier. "He's drunk again."

The second man nodded and both looked up at Mkombu's window.

They were Mkombu's personal guard. They were also his sons.

Inside the building, Jimbobwu Mkombu was finishing his second bottle of wine. When the bottle was empty, he smashed it against the wall, as he had done with the first, and opened a third bottle.

These fools, he thought. How could he hear anyone coming if they always babbled? Maybe he would have them shot in the morning. As he lifted the bottle of wine to his mouth, he wondered how it had gone wrong. Even though his men had been killed before they could eliminate the American Olympic team, things still had seemed to work out in Mkombu's favor. The world, never informed who was behind the planned murders, was infuriated with South Africa and Rhodesia, calling for a multinational force to enter both countries and overthrow the governments. Mkombu would soon be ruler.

And then this . . . this white avenger had appeared and Mkombu's world had turned upside down.

Suddenly, patrols began to disappear. Search parties never returned. An encampment was wiped out. Thirty men killed. No survivors. Then another encampment.

The story of the white avenger spread through the jungle like a summer fire. He was heading after Mkombu and Mkombu was frightened. What did he want?

They said he spoke of vengeance, but vengeance for what?

181

Mkombu drank more wine. He heard voices in his head, arguing.

When he finally arrives, offer him money, one voice said.

A spirit does not need money, a second voice said. *Offer him power.*

A spirit has power. Wealth and power can buy anyone.

Not a spirit, not an avenging spirit, not a white avenging spirit.

"Damn," snarled Mkombu and threw the bottle of wine against the wall, where it shattered. He watched the red wine run down the wall, spreading like blood from a wound.

"You down there," he shouted out the window.

"Yes, General," a voice answered.

"I want more men around the house. Many men. Men all around the house."

"That will take many men, General."

"I want many men, you idiot. Forty, fifty, no, sixty men, all around the house. Now hurry, you imbecile."

Mkombu went to the closet and took out his gunbelt and strapped it on. He made sure the .45 was loaded. He took out an automatic machine gun and made sure that it too was loaded. He hung grenades on his uniform for easy use.

When a knock came on the door, he almost pulled the pin on the grenade in his hand.

"Who is it?" he shrieked.

"The house is surrounded by men as you ordered."

"Idiot. Get out there with them where you belong," Mkombu shouted. "Make sure no one enters. No one, you hear?"

He sat in a chair facing the door with the machine gun across his lap.

Let him come, he thought, *let this white avenger come. We are ready for him.*

Into the night, he could hear widely spaced shots from outside, as his men shot at shadows, and with each shot he jumped. He felt hot and began to sweat under all the equipment he wore, but he kept it on. Better to be wet than dead. He regretted having broken his last bottle of wine.

He could go out and get one.

No. He would stay right here until morning. Right here, awake.

Five minutes later he was asleep.

Outside, sixty men ringed the small building.

The officer in charge of the detachment was talking to his second in command.

"It is the only way for us to stay alive," he said.

"I suppose," the second man agreed. "I will discuss it with the others." Ten minutes later, he returned and said, "Everyone agrees."

"It is the only way," said the officer in charge, and the two sons of Jimbobwu Mkombu looked at each other and nodded. The only way to live was to kill Mkombu. Then, when the white avenger came, he would find Mkombu dead and would have no reason to kill all of them.

"The only way," the second man agreed.

Mkombu awoke several times with a start, staring around the room in stark terror, firing his machine gun at shadows.

The walls of the bedroom were riddled with bullet holes. His dresser had pieces gouged out of it, and stuffing protruded from the mattress. But he was still alive.

For a moment he wondered if he really had anything to worry about. Those stories must be exaggerated. How could one man, one white man, be so awesome a force?

Impossible, he thought, crossing the room and peeking in the closet.

Preposterous, he told himself while he crouched down to peer under the bed.

He checked the locks on the windows and the door, then sat back down, fondling a grenade as if it were a woman's breast. Perhaps he needed a woman to relax him. And then perhaps these wild irrational fears would cease.

Outside, the officer in charge said, "It's time. We might as well get it over with."

"Who goes?" said the second officer.

"All of us," said the officer in charge.

"All sixty can't fit into the house."

The officer in charge thought about this for a moment. "All right, six of us will go in, but the others will stand in the hallway. They are part of it too."

"Of course. I'll stand in the hallway."

"You'll come with me," said the officer in charge to his brother. "Pick four more men."

A moment later, six of them were creeping up the steps toward Mkombu's bedroom.

Jimbobwu Mkombu heard a noise. He awoke but he could not move his head. He realized that he was paralyzed by fear. All these weapons he wore to protect himself and he was paralyzed by fear anyway.

It must have been a dream, he thought. *A terrifying dream. I'm dreaming that I can't move. Just wake up. Then I'll be all right. It's just a dream.*

When people are dreaming, do they know they are dreaming? He didn't know.

But then he remembered that, since boyhood, he had never dreamed.

He wasn't dreaming now.

With a monumental effort of will, he overcame his fear and turned his head.

And there in the shadow behind him, he saw a face. A white face.

He opened his mouth to cry out in terror, but no sound came out.

Outside Mkombu's door, the six soldiers held a convention. The door was locked and they were split three–three on kicking the door in, or knocking and trying to get Mkombu to open it by subterfuge.

"If I knock on the door, he probably won't start firing," said the officer in charge. This bit of logic started a landslide of votes toward knocking on the door, which eventually carried, six–zero.

The officer knocked.

Silence.

He knocked again.

Silence.

He knocked and called, "General." He paused, then called, "Father."

Silence.

"He knows why we're here," one of the other soldiers said.

The officer nodded. One last time. "General," he shouted, and when there was no answer, the six men threw their weight against the door and the flimsy wood gave way and the door swung open.

Jimbobwu Mkombu sat in a chair facing them. His eyes were wide open.

"I am sorry, Father, but we do not wish to die," the officer said.

"I'm sorry too, Father," said the second officer.

Mkombu did not move or speak.

"General?" the first man said.

The soldiers moved into the room and in the shadows they saw a piece of paper pinned to Mkombu's chest.

"The avenger," someone hissed.

"But how . . ."

The officer in charge walked toward Mkombu and as he reached out his hand to touch the note, he slightly jarred the body and Mkombu's head rolled off his shoulders, hit the floor with a bounce, and rolled along the floor until it came to a stop next to his pile of copies of *Playboy* magazine.

The soldiers screamed.

"He is dead," said the officer in charge. He plucked the note from Mkombu's chest.

"Can you read English?" he asked his brother.

"You're the lieutenant," his brother said. "I'm only a sergeant."

"I'm an African lieutenant. I don't have to read English."

"I read English," said one of the soldiers in the back.

"Here, read this," ordered the officer in charge.

The soldier looked at it several times, turning it often in his hand to make sure he had the words right side up.

"Well? What does it say?" demanded the officer.

"It says, 'Vengeance is mine.' It is signed . . ." and he peered closer at it to make sure he was reading it right.

"It is signed, 'Everyman.' "

CHAPTER NINETEEN

Chiun was still depressed but he seemed happy to be heading back to the United States on the British Airways plane.

"Russia is a land of barbarians," he said. "So is the United States, but at least the United States does not hold Olympic games there."

"They will in four years," Remo said.

Chiun looked at him.

"The '84 Olympics will be held in Los Angeles."

Chiun nodded. "Next time," he said, "we will not let that lunatic Smith talk us into entering just one event."

"Next time?" asked Remo.

"That's right," Chiun said. "And next time, I will accept no more excuses from you."

"Little Father," said Remo.

"Yes."

"In my heart, you'll always wear a gold medal," Remo said.

"Really?" said Chiun.

"Really," said Remo, feeling warm and expansive.

"I'm sure that will warm me in my old age as I starve to death," Chiun said. "Next time, you win a real gold medal."

"Whatever you say, Chiun."